Academic Library Use of eBooks

© 2014 Primary Research Group Inc.
Library of Congress Control Number: 2014951242
ISBN: 978-1-57440-308-4

Table of Contents

THE QUESTIONNAIRE..19
SURVEY PARTICIPANTS...26
SUMMARY OF MAIN FINDINGS...27
    Spending on Various Specific eBook Suppliers: Amazon 27
    Spending on Various Specific eBook Suppliers: OverDrive...27
    Spending on Various Specific eBook Suppliers: ebrary...27
    Spending on Various Specific eBook Suppliers: EBSCO 27
    Spending on Various Specific eBook Suppliers: Dawsonera..27
    Spending on Various Specific eBook Suppliers: Baker & Taylor 28
    Spending on Various Specific eBook Suppliers: EBL...28
    Spending on Various Specific eBook Suppliers: Ingram/Coutts/MyiLibrary...............................28
        Spending on Various Specific eBook Suppliers: Other Select Suppliers 28

    Spending on eBooks from Academic Presses...28
    Percentage of Total Books Ordered from Academic Presses that were eBooks 29
    Use of Public Domain eBook Sites by Academic Libraries..29
    Finding Aids for eBooks..29
    Format of EBooks 29
    Spending on eBook Aggregators vs. Individual Publishers...29
    eBook Spending Through Traditional Book Jobbers and Distributors...30
    Percentage of eBook Ordering through Electronic Information Aggregators not Connected to Major Book Jobbers or Distributors...30
    Percentage of eBook Orders Made Direct from Publishers..30
    Percentage of eBook Sales Made Through Consortia 31
    Academic Librarian Views of the eBook Options Offered by Academic Publishers 31
    Annual Growth Rate or eBook Use in Academic Libraries in the Past Year 31
    Academic Library Use eBook Procurement Models that Provide a Limited Number of Views for a Specified Price 32
    Academic Library Use eBook Procurement Models that Provide Unlimited Patron Use for a Specified Period of Time..32
    Academic Library Use eBook Procurement Models that Allows the Library to be the Perpetual Owner of a Title 32
    Annual Rate of Change in Spending on Various eBook Models...32
    Number of eBooks Owned Outright...33
    Spending on "Borrowing Rights" to eBooks 33
    Use of Tablet Computers in Academic Libraries...33
    The Percentage of eBooks in the Library Collection for which there is a Corresponding Print Copy..34
    Use of Endowed and other Special Funds for eBooks...34
    Extent of Use of eBooks for Course Reserve 34
    Academic Librarian View of Tendency of eBook Vendors to Resist Integration on Library Websites and Compel Use through the Supplier Website...34
    Spending on eDirectories...35

Views on Recent Level of Price Changes for eBooks..35
CHARACTERISTICS OF THE SAMPLE..36
Table 1.1 Your organization is Public or Private?...36
Table 1.2 Your organization is Public or Private? Broken out by College Type....................36
Table 1.3 Your organization is Public or Private? Broken out by FTE Enrollment..............36
Table 1.4 Your organization is Public or Private? Broken out by Annual Tuition Level...............36
Table 1.5 Your organization is Public or Private? Broken out by Carnegie Class.............37
Table 2.1 Full time equivalent enrollment for your institution is: 38
Table 2.2 Full time equivalent enrollment for your institution is: Broken out by College Type..38
Table 2.3 Full time equivalent enrollment for your institution is: Broken out by FTE Enrollment
....38
Table 2.4 Full time equivalent enrollment for your institution is: Broken out by Annual Tuition
Level 38
Table 2.5 Full time equivalent enrollment for your institution is: Broken out by Carnegie Class
....39
Table 3.1 The annual tuition ($) for your institution prior to any aid or deductions is:..............40
Table 3.2 The annual tuition ($) for your institution prior to any aid or deductions is: Broken
out by College Type...40
Table 3.3 The annual tuition ($) for your institution prior to any aid or deductions is: Broken
out by FTE Enrollment...40
Table 3.4 The annual tuition for your institution prior to any aid or deductions is: Broken out by
Annual Tuition Level..40
Table 3.5 The annual tuition ($) for your institution prior to any aid or deductions is: Broken
out by Carnegie Class 41
Table 4.1 Which phrase best describes your institution?..42
Table 4.2 Which phrase best describes your institution? Broken out by College Type 42
Table 4.3 Which phrase best describes your institution? Broken out by FTE Enrollment..........42
Table 4.4 Which phrase best describes your institution? Broken out by Annual Tuition Level ..43
Table 4.5 Which phrase best describes your institution? Broken out by Carnegie Class.............43
CHAPTER 2 – Basic Dimensions of EBook Use..44
Table 5 What is (will be) the library's total spending ($) on EBooks, including subscriptions,
downloads and other contract models for eBooks, in each of the following academic or calendar
years? Exclude spending on hardware..44
Table 5.1.1 What is (will be) the library's total spending ($) on EBooks, including
subscriptions, downloads and other contract models for eBooks, 2013-2014 academic or
calendar year? 44
Table 5.1.2 What is (will be) the library's total spending ($) on EBooks, including
subscriptions, downloads and other contract models for eBooks, 2013-2014 academic or
calendar year? Broken out by College Type...44
Table 5.1.3 What is (will be) the library's total spending ($) on EBooks, including
subscriptions, downloads and other contract models for eBooks, 2013-2014 academic or
calendar year? Broken out by FTE Enrollment..44
Table 5.1.4 What is (will be) the library's total spending ($) on EBooks, including
subscriptions, downloads and other contract models for eBooks, 2013-2014 academic or
calendar year? Broken out by Annual Tuition Level 45

Table 5.1.5 What is (will be) the library's total spending ($) on EBooks, including subscriptions, downloads and other contract models for eBooks, 2013-2014 academic or calendar year? Broken out by Carnegie Class 45
Table 5.2.1 What is (will be) the library's total spending ($) on EBooks, including subscriptions, downloads and other contract models for eBooks, 2014-15 (anticipated) academic or calendar year? 46
Table 5.2.2 What is (will be) the library's total spending ($) on EBooks, including subscriptions, downloads and other contract models for eBooks, 2014-15 (anticipated) academic or calendar year? Broken out by College Type 46
Table 5.2.3 What is (will be) the library's total spending ($) on EBooks, including subscriptions, downloads and other contract models for eBooks, 2014-15 (anticipated) academic or calendar year? Broken out by FTE Enrollment 46
Table 5.2.4 What is (will be) the library's total spending ($) on EBooks, including subscriptions, downloads and other contract models for eBooks, 2014-15 (anticipated) academic or calendar year? Broken out by Annual Tuition Level 46
Table 5.2.5 What is (will be) the library's total spending ($) on EBooks, including subscriptions, downloads and other contract models for eBooks, 2014-15 (anticipated) academic or calendar year? Broken out by Carnegie Class 47
Mention a few of your favorite eBook suppliers and why you like them. 48
Table 6 How much did your library spend ($) in the past year on eBooks or eDocuments from the following vendors? If you have not spent anything on eBooks from these vendors then put in "0" 50
Table 6.1.1 How much did your library spend ($) in the past year on eBooks or eDocuments from Amazon? 50
Table 6.1.2 How much did your library spend ($) in the past year on eBooks or eDocuments from Amazon? Broken out by College Type 50
Table 6.1.3 How much did your library spend ($) in the past year on eBooks or eDocuments from Amazon? Broken out by FTE Enrollment 50
Table 6.1.4 How much did your library spend ($) in the past year on eBooks or eDocuments from Amazon? Broken out by Annual Tuition Level 50
Table 6.1.5 How much did your library spend ($) in the past year on eBooks or eDocuments from Amazon? Broken out by Carnegie Class 51
Table 6.2.1 How much did your library spend ($) in the past year on eBooks or eDocuments from OverDrive? 52
Table 6.2.2 How much did your library spend ($) in the past year on eBooks or eDocuments from OverDrive? Broken out by College Type 52
Table 6.2.3 How much did your library spend ($) in the past year on eBooks or eDocuments from OverDrive? Broken out by FTE Enrollment 52
Table 6.2.4 How much did your library spend ($) in the past year on eBooks or eDocuments from OverDrive? Broken out by Annual Tuition Level 52
Table 6.2.5 How much did your library spend ($) in the past year on eBooks or eDocuments from OverDrive? Broken out by Carnegie Class 53
Table 6.3.1 How much did your library spend ($) in the past year on eBooks or eDocuments from 3M? 54
Table 6.3.2 How much did your library spend ($) in the past year on eBooks or eDocuments from 3M? Broken out by College Type 54

Table 6.3.3 How much did your library spend ($) in the past year on eBooks or eDocuments from 3M? Broken out by FTE Enrollment.. 54

Table 6.3.4 How much did your library spend ($) in the past year on eBooks or eDocuments from 3M? Broken out by Annual Tuition Level 54

Table 6.3.5 How much did your library spend ($) in the past year on eBooks or eDocuments from 3M? Broken out by Carnegie Class 55

Table 6.4.1 How much did your library spend ($) in the past year on eBooks or eDocuments from ebrary? 56

Table 6.4.2 How much did your library spend ($) in the past year on eBooks or eDocuments from ebrary? Broken out by College Type 56

Table 6.4.3 How much did your library spend ($) in the past year on eBooks or eDocuments from ebrary? Broken out by FTE Enrollment 56

Table 6.4.4 How much did your library spend ($) in the past year on eBooks or eDocuments from ebrary? Broken out by Annual Tuition Level 56

Table 6.4.5 How much did your library spend ($) in the past year on eBooks or eDocuments from ebrary? Broken out by Carnegie Class 57

Table 6.5.1 How much did your library spend ($) in the past year on eBooks or eDocuments from Dawsonera? 58

Table 6.5.2 How much did your library spend ($) in the past year on eBooks or eDocuments from Dawsonera? Broken out by College Type 58

Table 6.5.3 How much did your library spend ($) in the past year on eBooks or eDocuments from Dawsonera? Broken out by FTE Enrollment 58

Table 6.5.4 How much did your library spend ($) in the past year on eBooks or eDocuments from Dawsonera? Broken out by Annual Tuition Level 58

Table 6.5.5 How much did your library spend ($) in the past year on eBooks or eDocuments from Dawsonera? Broken out by Carnegie Class 59

Table 6.6.1 How much did your library spend ($) in the past year on eBooks or eDocuments from Knovel? 60

Table 6.6.2 How much did your library spend ($) in the past year on eBooks or eDocuments from Knovel? Broken out by College Type 60

Table 6.6.3 How much did your library spend ($) in the past year on eBooks or eDocuments from Knovel? Broken out by FTE Enrollment 60

Table 6.6.4 How much did your library spend ($) in the past year on eBooks or eDocuments from Knovel? Broken out by Annual Tuition Level 60

Table 6.6.5 How much did your library spend ($) in the past year on eBooks or eDocuments from Knovel? Broken out by Carnegie Class 61

Table 6.7.1 How much did your library spend ($) in the past year on eBooks or eDocuments from EBSCO/NetLibrary? 62

Table 6.7.2 How much did your library spend ($) in the past year on eBooks or eDocuments from EBSCO/NetLibrary? Broken out by College Type 62

Table 6.7.3 How much did your library spend ($) in the past year on eBooks or eDocuments from EBSCO/NetLibrary? Broken out by FTE Enrollment 62

Table 6.7.4 How much did your library spend ($) in the past year on eBooks or eDocuments from EBSCO/NetLibrary? Broken out by Annual Tuition Level 62

Table 6.7.5 How much did your library spend ($) in the past year on eBooks or eDocuments from EBSCO/NetLibrary? Broken out by Carnegie Class 63

Table 6.8.1 How much did your library spend ($) in the past year on eBooks or eDocuments from Baker&Taylor?...64

Table 6.8.2 How much did your library spend ($) in the past year on eBooks or eDocuments from Baker&Taylor? Broken out by College Type...64

Table 6.8.3 How much did your library spend ($) in the past year on eBooks or eDocuments from Baker&Taylor? Broken out by FTE Enrollment...64

Table 6.8.4 How much did your library spend ($) in the past year on eBooks or eDocuments from Baker&Taylor? Broken out by Annual Tuition Level..64

Table 6.8.5 How much did your library spend ($) in the past year on eBooks or eDocuments from Baker&Taylor? Broken out by Carnegie Class...65

Table 6.9.1 How much did your library spend ($) in the past year on eBooks or eDocuments from Blackwell?...66

Table 6.9.2 How much did your library spend ($) in the past year on eBooks or eDocuments from Blackwell? Broken out by College Type...66

Table 6.9.3 How much did your library spend ($) in the past year on eBooks or eDocuments from Blackwell? Broken out by FTE Enrollment..66

Table 6.9.4 How much did your library spend ($) in the past year on eBooks or eDocuments from Blackwell? Broken out by Annual Tuition Level...66

Table 6.9.5 How much did your library spend ($) in the past year on eBooks or eDocuments from Blackwell? Broken out by Carnegie Class..67

Table 6.10.1 How much did your library spend ($) in the past year on eBooks or eDocuments from Swets?..68

Table 6.11.1 How much did your library spend ($) in the past year on eBooks or eDocuments from EBL?..68

Table 6.11.2 How much did your library spend ($) in the past year on eBooks or eDocuments from EBL? Broken out by College Type...68

Table 6.11.3 How much did your library spend ($) in the past year on eBooks or eDocuments from EBL? Broken out by FTE Enrollment...68

Table 6.11.4 How much did your library spend ($) in the past year on eBooks or eDocuments from EBL? Broken out by Annual Tuition Level..68

Table 6.11.5 How much did your library spend ($) in the past year on eBooks or eDocuments from EBL? Broken out by Carnegie Class...69

Table 6.12.1 How much did your library spend ($) in the past year on eBooks or eDocuments from Ingram/Coutts/MyiLibrary?..70

Table 6.12.2 How much did your library spend ($) in the past year on eBooks or eDocuments from Ingram/Coutts/MyiLibrary? Broken out by College Type...70

Table 6.12.3 How much did your library spend ($) in the past year on eBooks or eDocuments from Ingram/Coutts/MyiLibrary? Broken out by FTE Enrollment...70

Table 6.12.4 How much did your library spend ($) in the past year on eBooks or eDocuments from Ingram/Coutts/MyiLibrary? Broken out by Annual Tuition Level...................................70

Table 6.12.5 How much did your library spend ($) in the past year on eBooks or eDocuments from Ingram/Coutts/MyiLibrary? Broken out by Carnegie Class...71

Table 6.13.1 How much did your library spend ($) in the past year on eBooks or eDocuments from Barnes & Noble?..72

Table 6.13.2 How much did your library spend ($) in the past year on eBooks or eDocuments from Barnes & Noble? Broken out by College Type...72

Table 6.13.3 How much did your library spend ($) in the past year on eBooks or eDocuments from Barnes & Noble? Broken out by FTE Enrollment..72

Table 6.13.4 How much did your library spend ($) in the past year on eBooks or eDocuments from Barnes & Noble? Broken out by Annual Tuition Level..72

Table 6.13.5 How much did your library spend ($) in the past year on eBooks or eDocuments from Barnes & Noble? Broken out by Carnegie Class 73

Table 6.14.1 How much did your library spend ($) in the past year on eBooks or eDocuments from Google? 74

Table 6.15.1 How much did your library spend ($) in the past year on eBooks or eDocuments from All academic presses?..74

Table 6.15.2 How much did your library spend ($) in the past year on eBooks or eDocuments from All academic presses? Broken out by College Type..74

Table 6.15.3 How much did your library spend ($) in the past year on eBooks or eDocuments from All academic presses? Broken out by FTE Enrollment 74

Table 6.15.4 How much did your library spend ($) in the past year on eBooks or eDocuments from All academic presses? Broken out by Annual Tuition Level...........................74

Table 6.15.5 How much did your library spend ($) in the past year on eBooks or eDocuments from All academic presses? Broken out by Carnegie Class 75

Does your library promote the use of any of the following to your library patrons (Internet Library, Project Gutenberg, HathiTrust,) and how 76

When you look to purchase an eBook how do you go about doing it? Which sources do you consult to check on eBook availability? 78

CHAPTER 3 – eBook Formats 80

Table 7.1 Approximately what percentage of the eBook titles your library offers are in PDF format?..80

Table 7.2 Approximately what percentage of the eBook titles your library offers are in PDF format? Broken out by College Type 80

Table 7.3 Approximately what percentage of the eBook titles your library offers are in PDF format? Broken out by FTE Enrollment...80

Table 7.4 Approximately what percentage of the eBook titles your library offers are in PDF format? Broken out by Annual Tuition Level 80

Table 7.5 Approximately what percentage of the eBook titles your library offers are in PDF format? Broken out by Carnegie Class..81

CHAPTER 4 – eBook Distribution 82

Table 8 What percentage of the library's total spending ($) on eBooks was with the following type of vendor: Aggregators, Individual Publishers? 82

Table 8.1.1 What percentage of the library's total spending ($) on eBooks was with Aggregators? 82

Table 8.1.2 What percentage of the library's total spending ($) on eBooks was with Aggregators? Broken out by College Type...82

Table 8.1.3 What percentage of the library's total spending ($) on eBooks was with Aggregators? Broken out by FTE Enrollment 82

Table 8.1.4 What percentage of the library's total spending ($) on eBooks was with Aggregators? Broken out by Annual Tuition Level 83

Table 8.1.5 What percentage of the library's total spending ($) on eBooks was with Aggregators? Broken out by Carnegie Class 83

Table 8.2.1 What percentage of the library's total spending ($) on eBooks was with Individual Publishers?...84

Table 8.2. What percentage of the library's total spending ($) on eBooks was with Individual Publishers? Broken out by College Type...84

Table 8.2.3 What percentage of the library's total spending ($) on eBooks was with Individual Publishers? Broken out by FTE Enrollment..84

Table 8.2.4 What percentage of the library's total spending ($) on eBooks was with Individual Publishers? Broken out by Annual Tuition Level..84

Table 8.2.5 What percentage of the library's total spending ($) on eBooks was with Individual Publishers? Broken out by Carnegie Class..85

Table 9 What percentage of the library's total eBook ordering was made through the following channels: 86

Table 9.1.1 What percentage of the library's total eBook ordering was made through eBook divisions of a traditional book jobber or book distributor such as EBSCO's NetLibrary, Ingram's MyiLibrary or Baker & Taylor's eBook Library and other such divisions?...................86

Table 9.1.2 What percentage of the library's total eBook ordering was made through eBook divisions of a traditional book jobber or book distributor such as EBSCO's NetLibrary, Ingram's MyiLibrary or Baker & Taylor's eBook Library and other such divisions? Broken out by College Type...86

Table 9.1.3 What percentage of the library's total eBook ordering was made through eBook divisions of a traditional book jobber or book distributor such as EBSCO's NetLibrary, Ingram's MyiLibrary or Baker & Taylor's eBook Library and other such divisions? Broken out by FTE Enrollment 86

Table 9.1.4 What percentage of the library's total eBook ordering was made through eBook divisions of a traditional book jobber or book distributor such as EBSCO's NetLibrary, Ingram's MyiLibrary or Baker & Taylor's eBook Library and other such divisions? Broken out by Annual Tuition Level...87

Table 9.1.5 What percentage of the library's total eBook ordering was made through eBook divisions of a traditional book jobber or book distributor such as EBSCO's NetLibrary, Ingram's MyiLibrary or Baker & Taylor's eBook Library and other such divisions? Broken out by Carnegie Class 87

Table 9.2.1 What percentage of the library's total eBook ordering was made through an electronic information aggregator not connected to a major book jobber or distributor?.......88

Table 9.2.2 What percentage of the library's total eBook ordering was made through an electronic information aggregator not connected to a major book jobber or distributor? Broken out by College Type...88

Table 9.2.3 What percentage of the library's total eBook ordering was made through an electronic information aggregator not connected to a major book jobber or distributor? Broken out by FTE Enrollment 88

Table 9.2.4 What percentage of the library's total eBook ordering was made through an electronic information aggregator not connected to a major book jobber or distributor? Broken out by Annual Tuition Level..88

Table 9.2. What percentage of the library's total eBook ordering was made through an electronic information aggregator not connected to a major book jobber or distributor? Broken out by Carnegie Class 89

Table 9.3.1 What percentage of the library's total eBook ordering was made direct from a publisher?... 90

Table 9.3.2 What percentage of the library's total eBook ordering was made direct from a publisher? Broken out by College Type 90

Table 9.3.3 What percentage of the library's total eBook ordering was made direct from a publisher? Broken out by FTE Enrollment... 90

Table 9.3.4 What percentage of the library's total eBook ordering was made direct from a publisher? Broken out by Annual Tuition Level 90

Table 9.3.5 What percentage of the library's total eBook ordering was made direct from a publisher? Broken out by Carnegie Class.. 91

Table 10.1 What percentage of the library's eBook collection spending is through contracts negotiated by a consortium?.. 92

Table 10.2 What percentage of the library's eBook collection spending is through contracts negotiated by a consortium? Broken out by College Type 92

Table 10.3 What percentage of the library's eBook collection spending is through contracts negotiated by a consortium? Broken out by FTE Enrollment.. 92

Table 10.4 What percentage of the library's eBook collection spending is through contracts negotiated by a consortium? Broken out by Annual Tuition Level 93

Table 10.5 What percentage of the library's eBook collection spending is through contracts negotiated by a consortium? Broken out by Carnegie Class... 93

CHAPTER 5 – eBook Circulation Figures.. 94

Table 11.1 What has been the growth rate of eBook use at your library in the past year, comparing if you can the last three months with the same period last year?................................ 94

Table 11.2 What has been the growth rate of eBook use at your library in the past year, comparing if you can the last three months with the same period last year? Broken out by College Type 94

Table 11.3 What has been the growth rate of eBook use at your library in the past year, comparing if you can the last three months with the same period last year? Broken out by FTE Enrollment 94

Table 11.4 What has been the growth rate of eBook use at your library in the past year, comparing if you can the last three months with the same period last year? Broken out by Annual Tuition Level 95

Table 11.5 What has been the growth rate of eBook use at your library in the past year, comparing if you can the last three months with the same period last year? Broken out by Carnegie Class.. 95

CHAPTER 6 – Purchasing Models 96

Table 12 What percentage of your library's eBook spending is accounted for by the following types of model?... 96

Table 12.1.1 What percentage of your library's eBook spending is accounted for by a model that provides a limited number of borrowings or circulations to patrons for a specified price 96

Table 12.1.2 What percentage of your library's eBook spending is accounted for by a model that provides a limited number of borrowings or circulations to patrons for a specified price Broken out by College Type 96

Table 12.1.3 What percentage of your library's eBook spending is accounted for by a model that provides a limited number of borrowings or circulations to patrons for a specified price Broken out by FTE Enrollment 96
Table 12.1.4 What percentage of your library's eBook spending is accounted for by a model that provides a limited number of borrowings or circulations to patrons for a specified price Broken out by Annual Tuition Level 97
Table 12.1.5 What percentage of your library's eBook spending is accounted for by a model that provides a limited number of borrowings or circulations to patrons for a specified price Broken out by Carnegie Class 97
Table 12.2.1 What percentage of your library's eBook spending is accounted for by subscriptions for unlimited patron use for a specified period of time 98
Table 12.2.2 What percentage of your library's eBook spending is accounted for by subscriptions for unlimited patron use for a specified period of time Broken out by College Type 98
Table 12.2.3 What percentage of your library's eBook spending is accounted for by subscriptions for unlimited patron use for a specified period of time Broken out by FTE Enrollment 98
Table 12.2.4 What percentage of your library's eBook spending is accounted for by subscriptions for unlimited patron use for a specified period of time Broken out by Annual Tuition Level 98
Table 12.2.5 What percentage of your library's eBook spending is accounted for by subscriptions for unlimited patron use for a specified period of time Broken out by Carnegie Class 99
Table 12.3.1 What percentage of your library's eBook spending is accounted for by an ownership model similar to print purchases of books where the library becomes the perpetual owner of the book as long as it is used only by recognized library patrons 100
Table 12.3.2 What percentage of your library's eBook spending is accounted for by an ownership model similar to print purchases of books where the library becomes the perpetual owner of the book as long as it is used only by recognized library patrons Broken out by College Type 100
Table 12.3.3 What percentage of your library's eBook spending is accounted for by an ownership model similar to print purchases of books where the library becomes the perpetual owner of the book as long as it is used only by recognized library patrons Broken out by FTE Enrollment 100
Table 12.3.4 What percentage of your library's eBook spending is accounted for by an ownership model similar to print purchases of books where the library becomes the perpetual owner of the book as long as it is used only by recognized library patrons Broken out by Annual Tuition Level 100
Table 12.3.5 What percentage of your library's eBook spending is accounted for by an ownership model similar to print purchases of books where the library becomes the perpetual owner of the book as long as it is used only by recognized library patrons Broken out by Carnegie Class 101
Table 12.4. What percentage of your library's eBook spending is accounted for by a pay per individual use where the library pays for each individual "check out" by patrons 102

Table 12.4.2 What percentage of your library's eBook spending is accounted for by a pay per individual use where the library pays for each individual "check out" by patrons Broken out by College Type..102

Table 12.4.3 What percentage of your library's eBook spending is accounted for by a pay per individual use where the library pays for each individual "check out" by patrons Broken out by FTE Enrollment 102

Table 12.4.4 What percentage of your library's eBook spending is accounted for by pay per individual use where the library pays for each individual "check out" by patrons Broken out by Annual Tuition Level...102

Table 12.4.5 What percentage of your library's eBook spending is accounted for by pay per individual use where the library pays for each individual "check out" by patrons Broken out by Carnegie Class 103

Table 13 Over the past year what has been the change in your spending in percentage terms on each of the following models: 104

Table 13.1.1 Over the past year what has been the change in your spending in percentage terms on a model that provides a limited number of borrowings or circulations to patrons for a specified price?...104

Table 13.1.2 Over the past year what has been the change in your spending in percentage terms on a model that provides a limited number of borrowings or circulations to patrons for a specified price? Broken out by College Type 104

Table 13.1.3 Over the past year what has been the change in your spending in percentage terms on a model that provides a limited number of borrowings or circulations to patrons for a specified price? Broken out by FTE Enrollment..104

Table 13.1.4 Over the past year what has been the change in your spending in percentage terms on a model that provides a limited number of borrowings or circulations to patrons for a specified price? Broken out by Annual Tuition Level...105

Table 13.1.5 Over the past year what has been the change in your spending in percentage terms on a model that provides a limited number of borrowings or circulations to patrons for a specified price? Broken out by Carnegie Class..105

Table 13.2.1 Over the past year what has been the change in your spending in percentage terms on subscriptions that allow unlimited patron use for a specified period of time?.........106

Table 13.2.2 Over the past year what has been the change in your spending in percentage terms on a subscription for unlimited patron use for a specified period of time? Broken out by College Type 106

Table 13.2.3 Over the past year what has been the change in your spending in percentage terms on a subscription for unlimited patron use for a specified period of time? Broken out by FTE Enrollment..106

Table 13.2.4 Over the past year what has been the change in your spending in percentage terms on a subscription for unlimited patron use for a specified period of time? Broken out by Annual Tuition Level...106

Table 13.2.5 Over the past year what has been the change in your spending in percentage terms on a subscription for unlimited patron use for a specified period of time? Broken out by Carnegie Class..107

Table 13.3.1 Over the past year what has been the change in your spending in percentage terms on an ownership model similar to print purchases of books where the library becomes the perpetual owner of the book as long as it is used only by recognized library patrons?...108

Table 13.3.2 Over the past year what has been the change in your spending in percentage terms on an ownership model similar to print purchases of books where the library becomes the perpetual owner of the book as long as it is used only by recognized library patrons? Broken out by College Type...108

Table 13.3.3 Over the past year what has been the change in your spending in percentage terms on an ownership model similar to print purchases of books where the library becomes the perpetual owner of the book as long as it is used only by recognized library patrons? Broken out by FTE Enrollment 108

Table 13.3.4 Over the past year what has been the change in your spending in percentage terms on an ownership model similar to print purchases of books where the library becomes the perpetual owner of the book as long as it is used only by recognized library patrons? Broken out by Annual Tuition Level...108

Table 13.3.5 Over the past year what has been the change in your spending in percentage terms on an ownership model similar to print purchases of books where the library becomes the perpetual owner of the book as long as it is used only by recognized library patrons? Broken out by Carnegie Class 109

Table 13.4.1 Over the past year what has been the change in your spending in percentage terms on a pay per individual use where the library pays for each individual "check out" by patrons?...110

Table 13.4.2 Over the past year what has been the change in your spending in percentage terms on a pay per individual use where the library pays for each individual "check out" by patrons? Broken out by College Type...110

Table 13.4.3 Over the past year what has been the change in your spending in percentage terms on a pay per individual use where the library pays for each individual "check out" by patrons? Broken out by FTE Enrollment..110

Table 13.4.4 Over the past year what has been the change in your spending in percentage terms on a pay per individual use where the library pays for each individual "check out" by patrons? Broken out by Annual Tuition Level..110

Table 13.4.5 Over the past year what has been the change in your spending in percentage terms on a pay per individual use where the library pays for each individual "check out" by patrons? Broken out by Carnegie Class..111

Table 14.1 Apart from works in the public domain, how many eBook titles does the library own outright through purchases from publishers or other vendors?..112

Table 14.2 Apart from works in the public domain, how many eBook titles does the library own outright through purchases from publishers or other vendors? Broken out by College Type...112

Table 14.3 Apart from works in the public domain, how many eBook titles does the library own outright through purchases from publishers or other vendors? Broken out by FTE Enrollment 112

Table 14.4 Apart from works in the public domain, how many eBook titles does the library own outright through purchases from publishers or other vendors? Broken out by Annual Tuition Level 113

Table 14.5 Apart from works in the public domain, how many eBook titles does the library own outright through purchases from publishers or other vendors? Broken out by Carnegie Class113

CHAPTER 7 – eBooks from Academic Presses...114

Table 15 What was (will be) the library's total spending ($) on eBooks from academic presses in the following years?..114

Table 15.1.1 What was (will be) the library's total spending ($) on eBooks from academic presses in 2013-14?..114
Table 15.1.2 What was (will be) the library's total spending ($) on eBooks from academic presses in 2013-14? Broken out by College Type...114
Table 15.1.3 What was (will be) the library's total spending ($) on eBooks from academic presses in 2013-14? Broken out by FTE Enrollment 114
Table 15.1.4 What was (will be) the library's total spending ($) on eBooks from academic presses in 2013-14? Broken out by Annual Tuition Level..114
Table 15.1.5 What was (will be) the library's total spending ($) on eBooks from academic presses in 2013-14? Broken out by Carnegie Class 115
Table 15.2.1 What was (will be) the library's total spending ($) on eBooks from academic presses in 2014-15 (anticipated)?...116
Table 15.2.2 What was (will be) the library's total spending ($) on eBooks from academic presses in 2014-15 (anticipated)? Broken out by College Type..................................116
Table 15.2.3 What was (will be) the library's total spending ($) on eBooks from academic presses in 2014-15 (anticipated)? Broken out by FTE Enrollment.......................116
Table 15.2.4 What was (will be) the library's total spending ($) on eBooks from academic presses in 2014-15 (anticipated)? Broken out by Annual Tuition Level..................116
Table 15.2.5 What was (will be) the library's total spending ($) on eBooks from academic presses in 2014-15 (anticipated)? Broken out by Carnegie Class 117
Table 16.1 About what percentage of the books that your library desires to order from academic presses are typically available as eBooks? 118
Table 16.2 About what percentage of the books that your library desires to order from academic presses are typically available as eBooks? Broken out by College Type....................................118
Table 16.3 About what percentage of the books that your library desires to order from academic presses are typically available as eBooks? Broken out by FTE Enrollment..............................118
Table 16.4 About what percentage of the books that your library desires to order from academic presses are typically available as eBooks? Broken out by Annual Tuition Level 119
Table 16.5 About what percentage of the books that your library desires to order from academic presses are typically available as eBooks? Broken out by Carnegie Class....................................119
Table 17.1 What percentage of the books that you order from academic presses do you order in an eBook format?...120
Table 17.2 What percentage of the books that you order from academic presses do you order in an eBook format? Broken out by College Type 120
Table 17.3 What percentage of the books that you order from academic presses do you order in an eBook format? Broken out by FTE Enrollment..120
Table 17.4 What percentage of the books that you order from academic presses do you order in an eBook format? Broken out by Annual Tuition Level 121
Table 17.5 What percentage of the books that you order from academic presses do you order in an eBook format? Broken out by Carnegie Class...121
What do you think of most of the eBook purchase options offered to you by academic publishers and how might they be altered? 122
CHAPTER 8 – EBooks in interlibrary loan 124
Table 18.1 Has the library ever used eBook rental or eBook interlibrary loan sites which enable patrons to have access to an eBook for a fee for a brief specified time period, often 30-60 days?
....124

Table 18.2 Has the library ever used eBook rental or eBook interlibrary loan sites which enable patrons to have access to an eBook for a fee for a brief specified time period, often 30-60 days? Broken out by College Type...124

Table 18.3 Has the library ever used eBook rental or eBook interlibrary loan sites which enable patrons to have access to an eBook for a fee for a brief specified time period, often 30-60 days? Broken out by FTE Enrollment 124

Table 18.4 Has the library ever used eBook rental or eBook interlibrary loan sites which enable patrons to have access to an eBook for a fee for a brief specified time period, often 30-60 days? Broken out by Annual Tuition Level...125

Table 18.5 Has the library ever used eBook rental or eBook interlibrary loan sites which enable patrons to have access to an eBook for a fee for a brief specified time period, often 30-60 days? Broken out by Carnegie Class 125

Table 19.1 How much did the library spend ($) exclusively on "borrowing rights" to eBooks defined as any model compels you to pay per time borrowed rather than unlimited rights or rights to a certain number of viewings for a set fee?..126

Table 19.2 How much did the library spend ($) exclusively on "borrowing rights" to eBooks defined as any model compels you to pay per time borrowed rather than unlimited rights or rights to a certain number of viewings for a set fee? Broken out by College Type.........................126

Table 19.3 How much did the library spend ($) exclusively on "borrowing rights" to eBooks defined as any model compels you to pay per time borrowed rather than unlimited rights or rights to a certain number of viewings for a set fee? Broken out by FTE Enrollment 126

Table 19.4 How much did the library spend ($) exclusively on "borrowing rights" to eBooks defined as any model compels you to pay per time borrowed rather than unlimited rights or rights to a certain number of viewings for a set fee? Broken out by Annual Tuition Level..........127

Table 19.5 How much did the library spend ($) exclusively on "borrowing rights" to eBooks defined as any model compels you to pay per time borrowed rather than unlimited rights or rights to a certain number of viewings for a set fee? Broken out by Carnegie Class 127

CHAPTER 9 – Who Uses What 128

In what areas is your library most anxious to build its eBook collection? 128

CHAPTER 10 – Use of Tablets in the Library..130

Table 20.1 Does the library loan out tablet computers to library patrons?.................................130

Table 20.2 Does the library loan out tablet computers to library patrons? Broken out by College Type...130

Table 20.3 Does the library loan out tablet computers to library patrons? Broken out by FTE Enrollment 130

Table 20.4 Does the library loan out tablet computers to library patrons? Broken out by Annual Tuition Level 131

Table 20.5 Does the library loan out tablet computers to library patrons? Broken out by Carnegie Class..131

Table 21.1 If so,what is the stock of tablet computers that the library maintains for loan?........132

Table 21.2 If so what is the stock of tablet computers that the library maintains for loan? Broken out by College Type..132

Table 21.3 If so what is the stock of tablet computers that the library maintains for loan? Broken out by FTE Enrollment..132

Table 21.4 If so what is the stock of tablet computers that the library maintains for loan? Broken out by Annual Tuition Level 132

Table 21.5 If so what is the stock of tablet computers that the library maintains for loan? Broken out by Carnegie Class 133

CHAPTER 11 – Print Vs Online 134

Table 22.1 For approximately what percentage of the eBooks in the library's collection would you estimate that the library also has a corresponding print copy? 134

Table 22.2 For approximately what percentage of the eBooks in the library's collection would you estimate that the library also has a corresponding print copy? Broken out by College Type 134

Table 22.3 For approximately what percentage of the eBooks in the library's collection would you estimate that the library also has a corresponding print copy? Broken out by FTE Enrollment 134

Table 22.4 For approximately what percentage of the eBooks in the library's collection would you estimate that the library also has a corresponding print copy? Broken out by Annual Tuition Level 135

Table 22.5 For approximately what percentage of the eBooks in the library's collection would you estimate that the library also has a corresponding print copy? Broken out by Carnegie Class 135

Table 23.1 If the library has an endowment, bequest, or specially dedicated fund of any kind for books, may this fund be used for the purchase of eBooks? 136

Table 23.2 If the library has an endowment, bequest, or specially dedicated fund of any kind for books, may this fund be used for the purchase of eBooks? Broken out by College Type 136

Table 23.3 If the library has an endowment, bequest, or specially dedicated fund of any kind for books, may this fund be used for the purchase of eBooks? Broken out by FTE Enrollment 137

Table 23.4 If the library has an endowment, bequest, or specially dedicated fund of any kind for books, may this fund be used for the purchase of eBooks? Broken out by Annual Tuition Level 137

Table 23.5 If the library has an endowment, bequest, or specially dedicated fund of any kind for books, may this fund be used for the purchase of eBooks? Broken out by Carnegie Class 138

CHAPTER 12 – EBooks and Electronic Course Reserve 139

Table 24.1 How would you describe your use of eBooks for course reserve? 139

Table 24.2 How would you describe your use of eBooks for course reserve? Broken out by College Type 139

Table 24.3 How would you describe your use of eBooks for course reserve? Broken out by FTE Enrollment 139

Table 24.4 How would you describe your use of eBooks for course reserve? Broken out by Annual Tuition Level 140

Table 24.5 How would you describe your use of eBooks for course reserve? Broken out by Carnegie Class 140

Over the past two years, the use of eBooks for electronic course reserves has increased or decreased? What are the 141

CHAPTER 13 – Statistics on EBook Use at the Library 142

In general how easy is it for you to obtain statistical data and develop reports on eBook use at your library? Is it as easy as for print books? 142

What measures has your library taken to develop easy to develop and easy to use reports on eBook use at your library? 144

Table 25.1 Some eBook vendors do not allow their products to be integrated into a library's systems but instead require that when an eBook link is clicked in a library catalog that the library patron be brought to the eBook vendor's platform in able to access the book. Which phrase describes your feelings about this?...145

Table 25.2 Some eBook vendors do not allow their products to be integrated into a library's systems but instead require that when an eBook link is clicked in a library catalog that the library patron be brought to the eBook vendor's platform in able to access the book. Which phrase describes your feelings about this? Broken out by College Type............................145

Table 25.3 Some eBook vendors do not allow their products to be integrated into a library's systems but instead require that when an eBook link is clicked in a library catalog that the library patron be brought to the eBook vendor's platform in able to access the book. Which phrase describes your feelings about this? Broken out by FTE Enrollment........................146

Table 25.4 Some eBook vendors do not allow their products to be integrated into a library's systems but instead require that when an eBook link is clicked in a library catalog that the library patron be brought to the eBook vendor's platform in able to access the book. Which phrase describes your feelings about this? Broken out by Annual Tuition Level............................147

Table 25.5 Some eBook vendors do not allow their products to be integrated into a library's systems but instead require that when an eBook link is clicked in a library catalog that the library patron be brought to the eBook vendor's platform in able to access the book. Which phrase describes your feelings about this? Broken out by Carnegie Class...........................148

CHAPTER 14 – EDirectories 149

Table 26.1 How much did the library in the past year spend ($) on electronic/internet versions of directories?..149

Table 26.2 How much did the library in the past year spend ($) on electronic/internet versions of directories? Broken out by College Type...149

Table 26.3 How much did the library in the past year spend ($) on electronic/internet versions of directories? Broken out by FTE Enrollment..149

Table 26.4 How much did the library in the past year spend ($) on electronic/internet versions of directories? Broken out by Annual Tuition Level..150

Table 26.5 How much did the library in the past year spend ($) on electronic/internet versions of directories? Broken out by Carnegie Class..150

Table 27.1 How much does the library plan to spend ($) on electronic/internet versions of directories in the upcoming year?..151

Table 27.2 How much does the library plan to spend ($) on electronic/internet versions of directories in the upcoming year? Broken out by College Type...151

Table 27.3 How much does the library plan to spend ($) on electronic/internet versions of directories in the upcoming year? Broken out by FTE Enrollment..151

Table 27.4 How much does the library plan to spend ($) on electronic/internet versions of directories in the upcoming year? Broken out by Annual Tuition Level.....................................152

Table 27.5 How much does the library plan to spend ($) on electronic/internet versions of directories in the upcoming year? Broken out by Carnegie Class..152

CHAPTER 15 – Pricing..153

Table 28 In the past year what has been the library's experience with changes in the prices of eBooks relative to the changes in price of traditional print books, online databases of full text articles, and other resources specified below?..153

Table 28.1.1 In the past year what has been the library's experience with changes in the prices of eBooks relative to print books?..153

Table 28.1.2 In the past year what has been the library's experience with changes in the prices of eBooks relative to print books? Broken out by College Type..............................153

Table 28.1.3 In the past year what has been the library's experience with changes in the prices of eBooks relative to print books? Broken out by FTE Enrollment......................153

Table 28.1.4 In the past year what has been the library's experience with changes in the prices of eBooks relative to print books? Broken out by Annual Tuition Level.................154

Table 28.1.5 In the past year what has been the library's experience with changes in the prices of eBooks relative to print books? Broken out by Carnegie Class........................154

Table 28.2.1 In the past year what has been the library's experience with changes in the prices of eBooks relative to online full text databases? 155

Table 28.2.2 In the past year what has been the library's experience with changes in the prices of eBooks relative to online full text databases? Broken out by College Type................155

Table 28.2.3 In the past year what has been the library's experience with changes in the prices of eBooks relative to online full text databases? Broken out by FTE Enrollment.........155

Table 28.2.4 In the past year what has been the library's experience with changes in the prices of eBooks relative to online full text databases? Broken out by Annual Tuition Level156

Table 28.2.5 In the past year what has been the library's experience with changes in the prices of eBooks relative to online full text databases? Broken out by Carnegie Class...........156

Table 29.1 What was the average percentage change in eBook prices that your organization paid in the last year? 157

Table 29.2 What was the average percentage change in eBook prices that your organization paid in the last year? Broken out by College Type..157

Table 29.3 What was the average percentage change in eBook prices that your organization paid in the last year? Broken out by FTE Enrollment 157

Table 29.4 What was the average percentage change in eBook prices that your organization paid in the last year? Broken out by Annual Tuition Level..158

Table 29.5 What was the average percentage change in eBook prices that your organization paid in the last year? Broken out by Carnegie Class 158

CHAPTER 16 – EBook Collection Planning..159

Discuss your library's eBook collection strategy. How fast do you expect your eBook collection to grow?..159

CHAPTER 17 – ETextbooks...163

THE QUESTIONNAIRE

CHAPTER 1 – Study Description & Demographics

1. Please provide the contact information requested below:

    A. Personal Name:
    B. Organization:
    C. Email Address:
    D. Phone Number:

2. Your organization is:

    A. Public College
    B. Private College
    C. Other (please specify)

3. Full time equivalent enrollment for your institution is:

4. The annual tuition for your institution prior to any aid or deductions is:

5. Which phrase best describes your institution?

    A. Community College
    B. 4Year College
    C. MA/PHD Granting Institution
    D. Research University

CHAPTER 2 – Basic Dimensions of EBook Use

6. What is (will be) the library's total spending ($) on EBooks, including subscriptions, downloads and other contract models for eBooks, in each of the following academic or calendar year? Exclude spending on hardware.

    A. 2013-2014
    B. 2014-2014 (anticipated)

7. Mention a few of your favorite eBook suppliers and why you like them.

8. How much did your library spend ($) in the past year on eBooks or eDocuments from the following vendors? If you have not spent anything on eBooks from these vendors then put in "0".

    A. Amazon
    B. OverDrive
    C. 3M
    D. ebrary
    E. Dawsonera
    F. Knovel
    G. EBSCO/NetLibrary
    H. Baker&Taylor
    I. Blackwell
    J. Swets
    K. EBL
    L. Ingram/Coutts/MyiLibrary
    M. Barnes & Noble
    N. Google
    O. All academic presses

9. Does your library promote the use of any of the following to your library patrons (Internet Library, Project Gutenberg, HathiTrust,) and how extensive is the use of these resources and other similar sites at your library??

10. When you look to purchase an eBook how do you go about doing it? Which sources do you consult to check on eBook availability?

CHAPTER 3 – eBook Formats

11. Approximately what percentage of the eBook titles your library offers are in PDF format?

CHAPTER 4 – eBook Distribution

12. What percentage of the library's total spending ($) on eBooks was with the following type of vendor:
    For example Amazon or NetLibrary would be considered aggregators while John Wiley & Sons would be an individual publisher.

    A. Aggregators (offer books from many publishers)
    B. Individual Publishers

13. What percentage of the library's total eBook ordering was made through the following channels:
    (We are asking who did you order from and pay the bill to)

    A. Through eBook divisions of a traditional book jobber or book distributor such as EBSCO's NetLibrary, Ingram's MyiLibrary or Baker & Taylor's eBook Library and other such divisions
    B. Through an electronic information aggregator not connected to a major book jobber or distributor
    C. direct from a publisher

14. What percentage of the library's eBook collection spending is through contracts negotiated by consortium?

CHAPTER 5 – eBook Circulation Figures

15. What has been the growth rate of eBook use at your library in the past year, comparing if you can the last three months with the same period last year?

CHAPTER 6 – Purchasing Models

16. What percentage of your library's eBook spending is accounted for by the following types of model?

    A. A model that provides a limited number of borrowings or circulations to patrons for a specified price
    B. A subscription for unlimited patron use for a specified period of time
    C. An ownership model similar to print purchases of books where the library becomes the perpetual owner of the book as long as it is used only by recognized library patrons
    D. A pay per individual use where the library pays for each individual "check out" by patrons

17. Over the past year what has been the change in your spending in percentage terms on each of the following models: (these answers should be some percentage of 100%)

    A. A model that provides a limited number of borrowings or circulations to patrons for a specified price

    B. Subscriptions that allow unlimited patron use for a specified period of time

    C. An ownership model similar to print purchases of books where the library becomes the perpetual owner of the book as long as it is used only by recognized library patrons

    D. A pay per individual use where the library pays for each individual "check out" by patrons

18. Apart from works in the public domain, how many eBook titles does the library own outright through purchases from publishers or other vendors? (this figure would exclude annual subscriptions and eBooks subject to limits on the number of times that they can be borrowed or viewed)

CHAPTER 7 – eBooks from Academic Presses

19. What was (will be) the library's total spending ($) on eBooks from academic presses in the following years?

    A. 2013-14

    B. 2014-15 (anticipated)

20. About what percentage of the books that your library desires to order from academic presses are typically available as eBooks?

21. What percentage of the books that you order from academic presses do you order in an eBook format (including those titles that you order in both print and eBook formats)

22. What do you think of most of the eBook purchase options offered to you by academic publishers and how might they be altered?

CHAPTER 8 – EBooks in Interlibrary Loan & Borrowing

23. Has the library ever used eBook rental or eBook interlibrary loan sites which enable patrons to have access to an eBook for a fee for a brief specified time period, often 30-60 days?

    A. Yes

    B. No

24. How much did the library spend ($) exclusively on "borrowing rights" to eBooks defined as any model compels you to pay per time borrowed rather than unlimited rights or rights to a certain number of viewings for a set fee?

CHAPTER 9 – Who Uses What

25. In what areas is your library most anxious to build its eBook collection?

CHAPTER 10 – Use of Tablets in the Library

26. Does the library loan out tablet computers to library patrons?

    A. Yes
    B. No
    C. No but in the works

27. If so what is the stock of tablet computers that the library maintains for loan?

CHAPTER 11 – Print Vs Online

28. For approximately what percentage of the eBooks in the library's collection would you estimate that the library also has a corresponding print copy?

29. If the library has an endowment, bequest, or specially dedicated fund of any kind for books, may this fund be used for the purchase of eBooks?

    A. Yes, we have a special endowment of other dedicated fund for books but we cannot use it for eBooks
    B. Yes, we have a special endowment or other dedicated fund for books and we can use it for eBooks
    C. Actually we have an endowment or fund especially for eBooks or other electronic/internet resources.
    D. No, we have no such endowment or dedicated fund for books of any kind

CHAPTER 12 – EBooks and Electronic Course Reserve

30. How would you describe your use of eBooks for course reserve?

    A. Not really used at all
    B. Scant use
    C. Used modestly
    D. Significant Use
    E. Accounts for more than half of all book use on Course Reserves

31. Over the past two years, the use of eBooks for electronic course reserves has increased or decreased? What are the current constraints on use and what do you expect for the near future?

CHAPTER 13 – Statistics on EBook Use at the Library

32. In general how easy is it for you to obtain statistical data and develop reports on eBook use at your library? Is it as easy as for database use? or for general book circulation data? How cooperative are eBook vendors in helping you to develop or access this data efficiently?

33. What measures has your library taken to develop easy to develop and easy to use reports on eBook use at your library?

34. Some eBook vendors do not allow their products to be integrated into a library's systems but instead require that when an eBook link is clicked in a library catalog that the library patron be brought to the eBook vendor's platform in able to access the book. Which phrase describes your feelings about this?

    A. It is natural that the publisher would want to retain some control
    B. It's slightly inconvenient but not really a problem for us
    C. It's problematic and we would like to see this changed soon
    D. It's a major issue for us and we have or might withhold

CHAPTER 14 – EDirectories

35. How much did the library in the past year spend on electronic/internet versions of directories?

36. How much does the library plan to spend on electronic/internet versions of directories in the upcoming year?

CHAPTER 15 – Pricing

37. In the past year what has been the library's experience with changes in the prices of eBooks relative to the changes in price of traditional print books, online databases of full text articles, and other resources specified below

    A. eBooks relative to print books
       i. Price increases have been about the same
      ii. Price increases have been higher for eBooks
     iii. Our eBook prices have not increased

    B. eBooks relative to online full text databases
       i. Price increases have been about the same
      ii. Price increases have been higher for eBooks
     iii. Our eBook prices have not increased

38. What was the average percentage change in eBook prices that your organization paid in the last year?

CHAPTER 16 – EBook Collection Planning

39. Discuss your library's eBook collection strategy. How fast do you expect your eBook collection to grow? Has it led to reduced spending on traditional books? Do your library patrons make use of eBook searching capacity? How will eBooks affect your cataloguing and information literacy strategies?

CHAPTER 17 – ETextbooks

40. Describe your library's attempts to license eTextbooks? Have you approached or negotiated with any textbook publishers over eBook rights? What kind of results have you achieved? Do you have plans or a strategy in this area?

SURVEY PARTICIPANTS

Australian National University Library
Bergen Community College
College of Staten Island/CUNY
Colorado School of Mines
Community College of Baltimore County
Community College of Philadelphia
Emerson College
Gulf Coast State College Library
Harvard Law School Library
International School of Creative Arts, UK
Jackson State Community College
Johns Hopkins University
Liberty University
Loyola Notre Dame Library
Mercer County Community College
Moffett Library Midwestern State University
Mount Saint Mary College
Mount St Joseph University
Muscatine Community College
Newcastle College
Northeastern State University
Okanagan College
Pfeiffer University
Richard Bland College Library
Saint Clair County Community College
Sam Houston State University
Simpson College
Southern New Hampshire University
Southwest Baptist University
Springfield Technical Community College
TCS Education System
University of Chichester
University of Rijeka Library
University of Wisconsin - La Crosse
University of Prince Edward Island

SUMMARY OF MAIN FINDINGS

Spending on Various Specific eBook Suppliers: Amazon

The libraries in the sample spent a median of nothing on eBooks from Amazon but one library spent as much as $15,000 and mean spending was $571, mostly driven by this outlier.

Spending on Various Specific eBook Suppliers: OverDrive

Spending on eBooks from OverDrive, a favorite in the public library market, was also modest, a mean of only $752, much of it determined by an outlier that spent $20,000.

Spending on Various Specific eBook Suppliers: ebrary

One dominant supplier was ebrary on which survey participants spent a mean of $14,201 and a median of $1,850. Private college libraries in the sample were particularly heavy spenders on ebrary, averaging $28,810 with a median of $5,014. Spending on ebrary rose dramatically with college size as libraries serving colleges with more than 7,000 students spent a mean of nearly $33,000 on ebrary while those at colleges with between 3,000 and 7,000 students spent $8,100 and those serving less than 3,000 spent only $1601. Libraries from colleges in the higher tuition range, more than $20,000 annually, also spent heavily on ebrary, a mean of more than $32,411.

Spending on Various Specific eBook Suppliers: EBSCO

Another dominant supplier was EBSCO on which libraries in the sample spent a mean of $7732 and a median of $1888. In contrast with ebrary, EBSCO was strongest in the public college market. Public colleges in the sample spent a mean of $9,225 on EBSCO eBooks while private colleges spent a mean of $4,447. EBSCO also did better among the lower tuition colleges. Colleges that charge less than $6,000 per year on tuition spent a mean of $14,400 and a median of $3,750 on EBSCO eBooks while those in the middle and highest tuition ranges spent substantially less, means of $2,741 and $4,941 respectively.

Spending on Various Specific eBook Suppliers: Dawsonera

Spending on Dawsonera was modest, averaging less than $35.00 per library. Spending on Knovel was higher, a mean of $1,089, with all spending by private college libraries with more than 7,000 students.

Spending on Various Specific eBook Suppliers: Baker & Taylor

The libraries in the sample spent a mean of $3,519 on eBooks from Baker and Taylor in the past year though median spending was 0. Baker and Taylor did much better in the community college/4-year college market than many other suppliers. Libraries sampled spent a mean of just $8.52 on eBooks from Blackwell and nothing on eBooks from Swets.

Spending on Various Specific eBook Suppliers: EBL

The libraries sampled spent a mean of $10,147 but a median of 0 on eBooks from EBL with most volume in the sample in the upscale private college market and one survey participant spending $250,000.

Spending on Various Specific eBook Suppliers: Ingram/Coutts/MyiLibrary

Ingram/Coutts/MyiLibrary saw mean spending of $552 with most spending accounted for by public colleges.

Spending on Various Specific eBook Suppliers: Other Select Suppliers

None of the libraries in the sample spent anything on eBooks from Google. Spending on eBooks from Barnes & Noble was a mean of $107. Spending on eBooks from 3M was minimal, a mean of must $3.45.

Spending on eBooks from Academic Presses

The spending patterns on eBooks from academic presses were curious. (Academic press is here defined as publishers that are controlled by or strongly associated with an institution of higher education as opposed to an academic publisher who may be a private publishers focused on the academic market.) Median spending was 0 as most libraries spent nothing on eBooks from these presses. However, a minority spent large amounts. Mean spending was $32,108 with an enormous difference between spending by public and private colleges in the sample; private colleges in the sample spent a mean of nearly $100,000 on eBooks from academic presses mostly from a few major players, one of which spent more than $742,000. Median spending for private colleges was only $6,500 suggesting that mega-deals allowing for access to very broad ranges of books account for much of this volume from a few major players. This spending appears ready to increase markedly as sample participants expected to spend a mean of $6.449 in 2014-5, up from a mean of $5,426 in 2013-14, or an increase of nearly 19%.

Percentage of Total Books Ordered from Academic Presses that were eBooks

A mean of 18.44% of titles ordered from academic presses were in an eBook format, including orders that call for both print and eBook versions. The larger the college, the more likely it was to order books from academic presses in an eBook format.

Use of Public Domain eBook Sites by Academic Libraries

We asked the libraries in the sample if they promoted use of public domain eBook sites and other sites that promote cost free or low cost eBook use and for the most part the libraries in the sample linked to such sites, included some catalog links, but found that use was low, and they made no strong efforts to promote use.

Finding Aids for eBooks

We asked the libraries how they went about looking for eBooks and here was not any real consensus. There is still nothing really similar to Books-in-Print and librarians tend to check their main supplier or several suppliers, as the case may be. EBSCO, YBP, ebrary and EBL were the most common sources and if this does not turn up the desired works then librarians tend to turn to individual publishers. YBP-GOBI was often used.

Format of EBooks

A mean of 68.83% of the eBook titles that the libraries in the sample offer are in PDF format. Public colleges were more likely than private ones to use the PDF format and a mean of close to 75% of their works were in the format vs only about 55% for private college libraries in the sample. Community colleges and 4-year colleges were a little more likely than research oriented institutions to offer titles in PDF format.

Spending on eBook Aggregators vs. Individual Publishers

The libraries in the sample spent a mean of 78.21% of their eBook spending acquiring books from aggregators rather than individual publishers. The median figure was 90%. The libraries in the sample reported that they obtained a mean of 18.45% of their eBooks from individual publishers; this leaves a residual of 3.34% that comes from neither aggregator nor publishers; it may be that these are public domain eBooks acquired by the library or the results of the library's own eBook or digitization program. Another explanation is that the term "aggregator" was not understood to include bookstores or that the term publisher was not thought to include some non-profits or government agencies not normally thought of in the restricted sense of the term "publisher". Spending on individual publishers as opposed to aggregators rose with FTE enrollment; it was higher among private than public colleges and much higher among colleges that charged more than $6,000 per year for tuition than among those that charged less than this amount. Community and 4-year colleges in the sample spent only a shade more than 9% of their eBook budgets with publishers while more research oriented colleges and universities spent 27.3% of the eBook spending directly with publishers.

eBook Spending Through Traditional Book Jobbers and Distributors

We also asked what percentage of a library's total eBook ordering was made through certain traditional book jobbers or book distributors and we specifically mentioned (but did not limit the question exclusively to) EBSCO, Ingram and Baker and Taylor.

A median of 50% and a mean of 48.53% of the eBook ordering done by the libraries in the sample was done through these types of organizations and their eBook arms. Admittedly this is a somewhat imprecise question as some major distributors have purchased traditional eBook aggregators but we feel that the question was generally properly understood to capture the presence in the academic eBook market of these traditional companies, dominant in the print market.

Percentage of eBook Ordering through Electronic Information Aggregators not Connected to Major Book Jobbers or Distributors

We then asked what percentage of the library's total eBook ordering was made through an electronic information aggregator not connected to a major book jobber or distributor. A mean of 30.32% of such orders were made through such aggregators but the median was only 7.5%. Admittedly, as we said, this was a question that could be plagued with imprecision since not all survey participants know the institutional affiliations of their suppliers. However, a minority appear to use aggregators not affiliated with the major print book distributors and to understand as much.

Percentage of eBook Orders Made Direct from Publishers

14.5% of eBook ordering was made direct from publishers rather than through aggregators. Private colleges made 22.4% of their eBook orders directly to publishers and colleges that charge more than $20,000 in tuition annually made 20.36% of their eBook orders directly from publishers. Also, the larger the college in terms of enrollment the more likely it was to order directly from publishers.

Percentage of eBook Sales Made Through Consortia

We also asked what percentage of a library's eBook collection spending was through contracts negotiated with a consortium. A mean of 30.69 and a median of 20% of eBook spending was through contracts negotiated thorough consortia. For private colleges in the sample, more than 38% of eBook spending is accounted for by contracts through consortia. For colleges with fewer than 3,000 students fte, nearly 41% of eBook spending is derived from consortia-negotiated contracts.

Academic Librarian Views of the eBook Options Offered by Academic Publishers

We asked the sampled libraries what they think of the eBook purchase options offered by academic publishers and unfortunately we used the "term" academic publisher rather than "academic press" as some survey participants pointed out. Nonetheless, most participants answered the question for its original intent: that of asking about academic presses. Their responses were instructive: most were frustrated with the eBook options of academic publishers, pointing out a dearth of package deals and poor pricing models.

This is despite the fact that – incredibly perhaps – a mean of only 28.64% of the books that libraries in the sample desire to order are perceived by them to be even available as eBooks. The median was 20% but the range here is somewhat suspicious – 0 to 75%. It may very well be that some academic libraries cannot find any of what they want to order from academic presses in eBook formats and that some can find three quarters of what they need in these formats. But it may also be that academic presses are doing a poor job of publicizing or distributing works in these formats, a reluctance that may come from fears that print sales will be undercut or simply with lack of familiarity with licensing models, or lack of access to aggregators.

Annual Growth Rate or eBook Use in Academic Libraries in the Past Year

We asked the colleges in the sample what had been the growth rate of eBook use at their library in the past year. One outlier said that growth had increased 900% and this drove the mean up to a dramatic 69.38%. However, median growth was "only" 15%. However, several libraries in the sample reported enormous increases over 100%. For libraries in colleges with more than 7,000 students, the mean increase was 62.2% and the median increase a still impressive 25%.

Academic Library Use eBook Procurement Models that Provide a Limited Number of Views for a Specified Price

We asked libraries in the sample what percentage of their eBook spending was accounted for by various kinds of payment models. The first we asked about was a model that provided a limited number of borrowings or other form of circulation control to patrons for a specified price. Most academic libraries did not purchase under this model but some used in exclusively so that median use was 0 but mean use was 26.24%. Libraries at colleges that charged tuition of less than $6,000 per year were much less likely than others to use this model.

Academic Library Use eBook Procurement Models that Provide Unlimited Patron Use for a Specified Period of Time.

We next asked about models which allow for unlimited patron use for a specified period of time. A mean of a drop more than 40% of the eBook spending by the libraries in the sample followed this model. However, use of this model dropped as enrollment rose; it accounted for approximately 51% of the eBook spending for libraries at colleges with enrollment of less than 3,000 but dropped to 41.825 for libraries at colleges with from 3,000 to 7,000 students and then dropped again to 27.55% for college libraries at colleges with more than 7,000 students.

Academic Library Use eBook Procurement Models that Allows the Library to be the Perpetual Owner of a Title

We also asked about ownership models similar to print purchases of books through which the library becomes the perpetual owner of the book as long as it is used only by recognized library patrons (so these models may contain some limitations on inter-library loan and are still often different from print book ownership). For the libraries in the sample, 28.58% of their purchases were through this type of model. This model was much more common for research-oriented colleges than for community and 4-year colleges.

Annual Rate of Change in Spending on Various eBook Models

We also asked about trends in spending on eBooks through different types of model. First, we asked about the annual percentage change in spending on models that provide a limited number of borrowings or circulation to patrons for a specified price. The annual increase in spending on this model was 19.57%; private colleges increased their spending on eBooks through this model by 26.67%.

The annual change in spending on eBooks through a model that grants unlimited patron use for a specified subscription period was a mean of 27.42% and a median of 10%. Spending growth through this model was greatest among small colleges with fewer than 3,000 students for which it grew by 40% in the past year. However, for the largest colleges, spending on eBooks through this model grew by only 8.64%. Also growth was highest among the low tuition colleges, with a growth rate of 38.18% for libraries of colleges that charge less than $6,000 per year in annual tuition.

Spending on the "ownership" model has been increasing at the median rate of 7.5% but since one outlier reported a 200% growth rate the mean rate of increase for the sample was nearly 26%. The pay per view model has been growing modestly, at 2.83% per year, but median growth was 0. Among the largest colleges, those with more than 7,000 students, growth was a little faster, a mean of 5.45% per year. All use was by the more research oriented colleges and universities.

Number of eBooks Owned Outright

We asked the libraries sampled how many eBooks do they own outright excluding those to which they subscribe and those subject to limits on the number of times that they can be viewed. The mean number of titles owned was 77,794 though the median was 11,000 and the range in the sample, from 0 to a maximum of 1,200,000. Private colleges in the sample owned many more eBook titles outright than did the public colleges, a mean of 173,042 for the former and 40,523 for the latter. Direct ownership of eBook titles also rose with the tuition charged by the college. Colleges that charge more than $20,000 annually for tuition had a mean of 179,708 eBook titles and a median of 55,000, far higher than the sample norms. Almost all of the ownership volume was accounted for by colleges offering advanced degrees or by universities.

Spending on "Borrowing Rights" to eBooks

Mean spending was $1,440 on models that compel the library to pay per time borrowed rather than unlimited rights or rights to a certain number of viewings or borrowings for a set fee. Median spending was 0 as most libraries in the sample did not use this model at all. Almost all spending on this model was by private colleges, mostly those with more than 7,000 students.

Use of Tablet Computers in Academic Libraries

Only 22.22% of the libraries in the sample loan out tablet computers to library patrons but another 11.11% say that such a program is "in the works". One third of private college libraries in the sample have a tablet lending program. The mean stock of tablets in the lending programs for the libraries in the sample was 7.36 with a median of 4 and a range of 0 to 35.

The Percentage of eBooks in the Library Collection for which there is a Corresponding Print Copy

We asked for what percentage of the library's eBooks in the library collection did the library also have a corresponding print copy. The libraries sampled had a corresponding print copy for a mean of 17.05% of the works in their eBook collection.

Use of Endowed and other Special Funds for eBooks

We asked whether or not endowed funds dedicated to building book collections could be used to purchase eBooks. We gave them three choices in this multiple choice question and the choices were: 1) Yes, we have a special endowment of other dedicated fund for books but we cannot use it for eBooks- 2) Yes, we have a special endowment or other dedicated fund for books and we can use it for eBooks- 3) No, we have no such endowment or dedicated fund for books of any kind.

47.22% of the libraries in the sample did not have any kind of endowment or dedicated fund for books of any kind; 8.33% did have a special endowment or fund for books but were unable to use it for eBooks; 30.56% had a special endowment or fund for eBooks and could use it for eBooks.

Extent of Use of eBooks for Course Reserve

We asked about the extent of use of eBooks for course reserve, offering four potential answers for this multiple choice question: 1) Not really used at all- 2)Scant use- 3)Used modestly- 4)Significant Use

33.33% said that eBooks were not used for course reserve at all; another 33.33% said that they received scant use; 11.11% said that they received modest use and only 8.33% said that they received significant use.

Academic Librarian View of Tendency of eBook Vendors to Resist Integration on Library Websites and Compel Use through the Supplier Website

We asked about the tendency of some eBook vendors to not allow their products to be integrated into a library system but instead require that when an eBook link is clicked in the library catalog that the library patron be brought to the eBook vendor's platform to be able to access the book. We gave the respondents four possible choices in this multiple choice question. The choices were: 1) It is natural that the publisher would want to retain some control.- 2) It's slightly inconvenient but not really a problem for us.- 3)It's problematic and we would like to see this changed soon.- 4) It's a major issue for us and we have or might withhold business from vendors that do it.

19.44% did not answer the question; 22.22% thought that it was natural that the publisher would want to retain some control and another 25% said that it was slightly inconvenient but not really a problem; another 5.56% considered it problematic and would like to see this changed soon. For 27.78%, it was a major issue and they might withhold business from vendors that do it. This last answer was particularly common among private colleges, of which 41.67% gave this response. Half of all colleges that charge more than $20,000 per year for tuition gave this answer.

Spending on eDirectories

The libraries in the sample spent a mean of $2260 on electronic versions of directories; median spending was 0 and the range was 0 to $25,079. Almost all volume was with colleges that offer advanced degrees or universities.

Views on Recent Level of Price Changes for eBooks

We asked the sample what had been their experience with price increases for eBooks in the past year relative to their experience with other mediums such as print books or databases. First we asked how eBook price changes compared to those for print books. We gave them three choices: 1) Price increases have been about the same- 2) Price increases have been higher for eBooks- 3) Our eBook prices have not increased.

For close to 39% of survey participants price increases for eBooks and print books have been about the same while 30.56% believe that price increases for eBooks have been higher and 8.33% say that their eBook prices have not increased. The median increase in eBook prices reported by the libraries in the sample was 5% though the mean was much higher, 9.19%, as one survey participant reported a 45% increase.

CHARACTERISTICS OF THE SAMPLE

Table 1.1 Your organization is Public or Private?

	No Answer	Public College	Private College
Entire sample	0,00%	66,67%	33,33%

Table 1.2 Your organization is Public or Private? Broken out by College Type

College Type	Public College	Private College
Public	100,00%	0,00%
Private	0,00%	100,00%

Table 1.3 Your organization is Public or Private? Broken out by FTE Enrollment

FTE Enrollment	Public College	Private College
less than 3000	58,33%	41,67%
3000 - 7000	75,00%	25,00%
more than 7000	66,67%	33,33%

Table 1.4 Your organization is Public or Private? Broken out by Annual Tuition Level

Annual Tuition Level	Public College	Private College
less than $6000	100,00%	0,00%
$6000 - $20000	91,67%	8,33%
more than $20000	8,33%	91,67%

Table 1.5 Your organization is Public or Private? Broken out by Carnegie Class

Carnegie Class	Public College	Private College
Community College / 4-Year College	82,35%	17,65%
MA/PHD Granting / Research University	52,63%	47,37%

Table 2.1 Full time equivalent enrollment for your institution is:

	Mean	Median	Minimum	Maximum
Entire sample	7923,94	5100,00	28,00	60670,00

Table 2.2 Full time equivalent enrollment for your institution is: Broken out by College Type

College Type	Mean	Median	Minimum	Maximum
Public	6623,83	5450,00	28,00	20000,00
Private	10524,17	3600,00	1600,00	60670,00

Table 2.3 Full time equivalent enrollment for your institution is: Broken out by FTE Enrollment

FTE Enrollment	Mean	Median	Minimum	Maximum
less than 3000	1774,42	1729,50	28,00	2890,00
3000 - 7000	5014,67	5100,00	3200,00	6996,00
more than 7000	16982,75	14026,50	7337,00	60670,00

Table 2.4 Full time equivalent enrollment for your institution is: Broken out by Annual Tuition Level

Annual Tuition Level	Mean	Median	Minimum	Maximum
less than $6000	4896,92	4450,00	28,00	14890,00
$6000 - $20000	8025,75	7520,50	700,00	20000,00
more than $20000	10849,17	4750,00	1659,00	60670,00

Table 2.5 Full time equivalent enrollment for your institution is: Broken out by Carnegie Class

Carnegie Class	Mean	Median	Minimum	Maximum
Community College / 4-Year College	5001,29	4000,00	700,00	15106,00
MA/PHD Granting / Research University	10538,95	6500,00	28,00	60670,00

Table 3.1 The annual tuition ($) for your institution prior to any aid or deductions is:

	Mean	Median	Minimum	Maximum
Entire sample	17494,81	14105,50	800,00	53308,00

Table 3.2 The annual tuition ($) for your institution prior to any aid or deductions is: Broken out by College Type

College Type	Mean	Median	Minimum	Maximum
Public	8883,08	5750,00	800,00	29500,00
Private	34718,25	33275,00	20000,00	53308,00

Table 3.3 The annual tuition ($) for your institution prior to any aid or deductions is: Broken out by FTE Enrollment

FTE Enrollment	Mean	Median	Minimum	Maximum
less than 3000	17887,17	16900,00	800,00	53308,00
3000 - 7000	16896,58	9785,50	3000,00	50000,00
more than 7000	17700,67	12436,00	1250,00	48000,00

Table 3.4 The annual tuition for your institution prior to any aid or deductions is: Broken out by Annual Tuition Level

Annual Tuition Level	Mean	Median	Minimum	Maximum
less than $6000	3428,83	3544,00	800,00	5500,00
$6000 - $20000	13545,67	14105,50	6000,00	20000,00
more than $20000	35509,92	33275,00	20300,00	53308,00

Table 3.5 The annual tuition ($) for your institution prior to any aid or deductions is: Broken out by Carnegie Class

Carnegie Class	Mean	Median	Minimum	Maximum
Community College / 4-Year College	12871,82	7000,00	800,00	50000,00
MA/PHD Granting / Research University	21631,16	20000,00	1250,00	53308,00

Table 4.1 Which phrase best describes your institution?

	Community College	4Year College	MA/PHD Granting Institution	Research University
Entire sample	38,89%	8,33%	38,89%	13,89%

Table 4.2 Which phrase best describes your institution? Broken out by College Type

College Type	Community College	4Year College	MA/PHD Granting Institution	Research University
Public	58,33%	0,00%	25,00%	16,67%
Private	0,00%	25,00%	66,67%	8,33%

Table 4.3 Which phrase best describes your institution? Broken out by FTE Enrollment

FTE Enrollment	Community College	4Year College	MA/PHD Granting Institution	Research University
less than 3000	50,00%	8,33%	33,33%	8,33%
3000 - 7000	41,67%	16,67%	33,33%	8,33%
more than 7000	25,00%	0,00%	50,00%	25,00%

Table 4.4 Which phrase best describes your institution? Broken out by Annual Tuition Level

Annual Tuition Level	Community College	4Year College	MA/PHD Granting Institution	Research University
less than $6000	66,67%	0,00%	16,67%	16,67%
$6000 - $20000	50,00%	0,00%	33,33%	16,67%
more than $20000	0,00%	25,00%	66,67%	8,33%

Table 4.5 Which phrase best describes your institution? Broken out by Carnegie Class

Carnegie Class	Community College	4Year College	MA/PHD Granting Institution	Research University
Community College / 4-Year College	82,35%	17,65%	0,00%	0,00%
MA/PHD Granting / Research University	0,00%	0,00%	73,68%	26,32%

CHAPTER 2 – Basic Dimensions of EBook Use

Table 5 What is (will be) the library's total spending ($) on EBooks, including subscriptions, downloads and other contract models for eBooks, in each of the following academic or calendar years? Exclude spending on hardware.

Table 5.1.1 What is (will be) the library's total spending ($) on EBooks, including subscriptions, downloads and other contract models for eBooks, 2013-2014 academic or calendar year?

	Mean	Median	Minimum	Maximum
Entire sample	68623,06	20000,00	0,00	1019637,00

Table 5.1.2 What is (will be) the library's total spending ($) on EBooks, including subscriptions, downloads and other contract models for eBooks, 2013-2014 academic or calendar year? Broken out by College Type

College Type	Mean	Median	Minimum	Maximum
Public	28288,62	15000,00	0,00	200000,00
Private	145625,18	30000,00	0,00	1019637,00

Table 5.1.3 What is (will be) the library's total spending ($) on EBooks, including subscriptions, downloads and other contract models for eBooks, 2013-2014 academic or calendar year? Broken out by FTE Enrollment

FTE Enrollment	Mean	Median	Minimum	Maximum
less than 3000	9719,92	4000,00	0,00	39576,00
3000 - 7000	21801,50	17500,00	6000,00	50000,00
more than 7000	186128,40	47973,50	10000,00	1019637,00

Table 5.1.4 What is (will be) the library's total spending ($) on EBooks, including subscriptions, downloads and other contract models for eBooks, 2013-2014 academic or calendar year? Broken out by Annual Tuition Level

Annual Tuition Level	Mean	Median	Minimum	Maximum
less than $6000	29537,17	10550,00	0,00	200000,00
$6000 - $20000	23961,50	22957,50	0,00	60000,00
more than $20000	160187,70	34788,00	2717,00	1019637,00

Table 5.1.5 What is (will be) the library's total spending ($) on EBooks, including subscriptions, downloads and other contract models for eBooks, 2013-2014 academic or calendar year? Broken out by Carnegie Class

Carnegie Class	Mean	Median	Minimum	Maximum
Community College / 4-Year College	11551,06	10000,00	0,00	44000,00
MA/PHD Granting / Research University	125695,06	40288,00	0,00	1019637,00

Table 5.2.1 What is (will be) the library's total spending ($) on EBooks, including subscriptions, downloads and other contract models for eBooks, 2014-15 (anticipated) academic or calendar year?

	Mean	Median	Minimum	Maximum
Entire sample	79360,16	26707,50	0,00	1100000,00

Table 5.2.2 What is (will be) the library's total spending ($) on EBooks, including subscriptions, downloads and other contract models for eBooks, 2014-15 (anticipated) academic or calendar year? Broken out by College Type

College Type	Mean	Median	Minimum	Maximum
Public	37298,81	20000,00	0,00	350000,00
Private	159659,09	35000,00	250,00	1100000,00

Table 5.2.3 What is (will be) the library's total spending ($) on EBooks, including subscriptions, downloads and other contract models for eBooks, 2014-15 (anticipated) academic or calendar year? Broken out by FTE Enrollment

FTE Enrollment	Mean	Median	Minimum	Maximum
less than 3000	12050,83	6500,00	0,00	45000,00
3000 - 7000	25691,50	20957,50	7000,00	60000,00
more than 7000	213800,00	53000,00	20000,00	1100000,00

Table 5.2.4 What is (will be) the library's total spending ($) on EBooks, including subscriptions, downloads and other contract models for eBooks, 2014-15 (anticipated) academic or calendar year? Broken out by Annual Tuition Level

Annual Tuition Level	Mean	Median	Minimum	Maximum
less than $6000	44321,67	12180,00	0,00	350000,00
$6000 - $20000	25166,50	26707,50	0,00	60000,00
more than $20000	175600,00	40000,00	3000,00	1100000,00

Table 5.2.5 What is (will be) the library's total spending ($) on EBooks, including subscriptions, downloads and other contract models for eBooks, 2014-15 (anticipated) academic or calendar year? Broken out by Carnegie Class

Carnegie Class	Mean	Median	Minimum	Maximum
Community College / 4-Year College	14375,00	10250,00	0,00	46000,00
MA/PHD Granting / Research University	144345,31	41000,00	250,00	1100000,00

Mention a few of your favorite eBook suppliers and why you like them.

1) We only purchase EBSCO eBook collections at this time
2) Books@Ovid - subject selection EBSCO - buying individual titles as needed
3) EBSCO--good search interface; good selection process
4) ebrary. wide number of titles and currency
5) EBSCO,
6) Suppliers without DRM, because easier usage.
7) EBSCO academic subscription: range of publishers and subject matter. ebrary international academic subscription: range of publishers and subject matter; the representatives are honest and reliable withe queries, troubleshooting etc.
8) Gale - we mostly collect reference eBooks and they make it easy to find the titles we normally carry in print, but are now available electronically
9) MyiLibrary -- main print jobber so easy to select eBook if it is available instead of print plus we have PDA, EBSCO -- excellent search interface and soon will have PDA (plus a benefit that it is discoverable in EBSCO databases); both are discoverable in our catalog and through the discovery tool
10) Overdrive
11) ebrary - their subscription platform is very good and crosses all disciplines
12) None used
13) Springer - unlimited access and no DRM, print on demand service, no DRM, and did I mention no DRM, no stupid "checking the book out model" Unlimited access and no DRM
14) ebrary and EBL have been robustly adopted by our users, and the intuitive nature of their interface complements nicely the considerable overlap with our areas of focus supported by their collections
15) ebrary Salem Cambridge Gale EBSCO e-books
16) DawsonEra - ability to order individual e-books with a same-day turnaround. ebrary - on-tap access to 70,000 volume elibrary.
17) Coutts – platform\
18) Brill - good content Oxford University Press - good content
19) EBSCOhost
20) EBSCO - no future hosting fees, easy platform to use EBL - non-linear lending price model
21) ebrary, EBSCO, Safari,
22) ebsco - easy to use existing vendor, variety of publishers, PDA ebrary - variety of publishers, PDA gale - PDA, right reading level for community college students
23) Springer. Their policies allow unlimited downloading and printing. Knovel: Fit our student's needs very well 24x7, McGraw-Hill engineering.
24) EBSCO because competitive prices
25) ProQuest has ebrary and is very comprehensive.

26) ebrary Academic Collection- good selection- subscription EBSCO Academic Collection- good selection subscription STAT REF- good nursing books with mobile applications Safari. About 150 computer books

27) EBSCO and ebrary. Both have made efforts to offer seamless access, integration into library systems simple, and downloadable access.

28) EBL - created a DDA program (great selection of publishers) helps our ILL service. Springer - while they spread major reference titles over a number of year and that requires purchasing multiple years (can be expensive), we still like their non -DRM model.

29) ebrary - subscription collections are tremendous; multiuser model is really the only acceptable one for e-books in my opinion (making eBooks behave like physical books is the business model of dinosaurs) EBSCO - subscription collections are also very good & complements ebrary (& vice versa) Springer - extensive catalog at low cost with no DRM hoops; should be helping them more than it is.

30) We have a patron-driven acquisition program with ebrary, and we have invested heavily in that. We prefer aggregators so that we have fewer licenses and interfaces to manage. But we do also purchase direct. We have a lot of content from Oxford, including Oxford Scholarship Online, Oxford Biblical Studies, Oxford Reference Online, etc. We also have a lot of Cambridge content through the Companions.

31) EBL - Patron driven acquisition ebrary - good selection EBSCO - familiar interface

32) Rittenhouse--easy purchase and implementation EBSCO--same interface as DBs and staff, students, and faculty prefer EBSCO interface to ProQuest

33) ebrary - their PDA model works very well for us. EBSCO - their subscription package enabled us to quickly increase our eBook offerings.

Table 6 How much did your library spend ($) in the past year on eBooks or eDocuments from the following vendors? If you have not spent anything on eBooks from these vendors then put in "0".

Table 6.1.1 How much did your library spend ($) in the past year on eBooks or eDocuments from Amazon?

	Mean	Median	Minimum	Maximum
Entire sample	517,24	0,00	0,00	15000,00

Table 6.1.2 How much did your library spend ($) in the past year on eBooks or eDocuments from Amazon? Broken out by College Type

College Type	Mean	Median	Minimum	Maximum
Public	0,00	0,00	0,00	0,00
Private	1875,00	0,00	0,00	15000,00

Table 6.1.3 How much did your library spend ($) in the past year on eBooks or eDocuments from Amazon? Broken out by FTE Enrollment

FTE Enrollment	Mean	Median	Minimum	Maximum
less than 3000	0,00	0,00	0,00	0,00
3000 - 7000	1363,64	0,00	0,00	15000,00
more than 7000	0,00	0,00	0,00	0,00

Table 6.1.4 How much did your library spend ($) in the past year on eBooks or eDocuments from Amazon? Broken out by Annual Tuition Level

Annual Tuition Level	Mean	Median	Minimum	Maximum
less than $6000	0,00	0,00	0,00	0,00
$6000 - $20000	0,00	0,00	0,00	0,00
more than $20000	2142,86	0,00	0,00	15000,00

Table 6.1.5 How much did your library spend ($) in the past year on eBooks or eDocuments from Amazon? Broken out by Carnegie Class

Carnegie Class	Mean	Median	Minimum	Maximum
Community College / 4-Year College	0,00	0,00	0,00	0,00
MA/PHD Granting / Research University	1071,43	0,00	0,00	15000,00

Table 6.2.1 How much did your library spend ($) in the past year on eBooks or eDocuments from OverDrive?

	Mean	Median	Minimum	Maximum
Entire sample	752,37	0,00	0,00	20000,00

Table 6.2.2 How much did your library spend ($) in the past year on eBooks or eDocuments from OverDrive? Broken out by College Type

College Type	Mean	Median	Minimum	Maximum
Public	121,24	0,00	0,00	2300,00
Private	2225,00	0,00	0,00	20000,00

Table 6.2.3 How much did your library spend ($) in the past year on eBooks or eDocuments from OverDrive? Broken out by FTE Enrollment

FTE Enrollment	Mean	Median	Minimum	Maximum
less than 3000	2249,56	0,00	0,00	20000,00
3000 - 7000	211,36	0,00	0,00	2300,00
more than 7000	0,00	0,00	0,00	0,00

Table 6.2.4 How much did your library spend ($) in the past year on eBooks or eDocuments from OverDrive? Broken out by Annual Tuition Level

Annual Tuition Level	Mean	Median	Minimum	Maximum
less than $6000	231,45	0,00	0,00	2300,00
$6000 - $20000	0,00	0,00	0,00	0,00
more than $20000	2503,13	0,00	0,00	20000,00

Table 6.2.5 How much did your library spend ($) in the past year on eBooks or eDocuments from OverDrive? Broken out by Carnegie Class

Carnegie Class	Mean	Median	Minimum	Maximum
Community College / 4-Year College	171,40	0,00	0,00	2300,00
MA/PHD Granting / Research University	1333,33	0,00	0,00	20000,00

Table 6.3.1 How much did your library spend ($) in the past year on eBooks or eDocuments from 3M?

	Mean	Median	Minimum	Maximum
Entire sample	3,45	0,00	0,00	100,00

Table 6.3.2 How much did your library spend ($) in the past year on eBooks or eDocuments from 3M? Broken out by College Type

College Type	Mean	Median	Minimum	Maximum
Public	0,00	0,00	0,00	0,00
Private	12,50	0,00	0,00	100,00

Table 6.3.3 How much did your library spend ($) in the past year on eBooks or eDocuments from 3M? Broken out by FTE Enrollment

FTE Enrollment	Mean	Median	Minimum	Maximum
less than 3000	0,00	0,00	0,00	0,00
3000 - 7000	9,09	0,00	0,00	100,00
more than 7000	0,00	0,00	0,00	0,00

Table 6.3.4 How much did your library spend ($) in the past year on eBooks or eDocuments from 3M? Broken out by Annual Tuition Level

Annual Tuition Level	Mean	Median	Minimum	Maximum
less than $6000	0,00	0,00	0,00	0,00
$6000 - $20000	0,00	0,00	0,00	0,00
more than $20000	14,29	0,00	0,00	100,00

Table 6.3.5 How much did your library spend ($) in the past year on eBooks or eDocuments from 3M? Broken out by Carnegie Class

Carnegie Class	Mean	Median	Minimum	Maximum
Community College / 4-Year College	6,67	0,00	0,00	100,00
MA/PHD Granting / Research University	0,00	0,00	0,00	0,00

Table 6.4.1 How much did your library spend ($) in the past year on eBooks or eDocuments from ebrary?

	Mean	Median	Minimum	Maximum
Entire sample	14209,63	1850,00	0,00	200000,00

Table 6.4.2 How much did your library spend ($) in the past year on eBooks or eDocuments from ebrary? Broken out by College Type

College Type	Mean	Median	Minimum	Maximum
Public	7952,38	0,00	0,00	65000,00
Private	28809,89	5014,00	0,00	200000,00

Table 6.4.3 How much did your library spend ($) in the past year on eBooks or eDocuments from ebrary? Broken out by FTE Enrollment

FTE Enrollment	Mean	Median	Minimum	Maximum
less than 3000	1601,40	0,00	0,00	6000,00
3000 - 7000	8100,00	6500,00	0,00	20000,00
more than 7000	32927,50	5100,00	0,00	200000,00

Table 6.4.4 How much did your library spend ($) in the past year on eBooks or eDocuments from ebrary? Broken out by Annual Tuition Level

Annual Tuition Level	Mean	Median	Minimum	Maximum
less than $6000	9318,18	3500,00	0,00	65000,00
$6000 - $20000	5863,64	0,00	0,00	35000,00
more than $20000	32411,13	10007,00	0,00	200000,00

Table 6.4.5 How much did your library spend ($) in the past year on eBooks or eDocuments from ebrary? Broken out by Carnegie Class

Carnegie Class	Mean	Median	Minimum	Maximum
Community College / 4-Year College	3035,71	0,00	0,00	15000,00
MA/PHD Granting / Research University	23986,81	7507,00	0,00	200000,00

Table 6.5.1 How much did your library spend ($) in the past year on eBooks or eDocuments from Dawsonera?

	Mean	Median	Minimum	Maximum
Entire sample	34,48	0,00	0,00	1000,00

Table 6.5.2 How much did your library spend ($) in the past year on eBooks or eDocuments from Dawsonera? Broken out by College Type

College Type	Mean	Median	Minimum	Maximum
Public	47,62	0,00	0,00	1000,00
Private	0,00	0,00	0,00	0,00

Table 6.5.3 How much did your library spend ($) in the past year on eBooks or eDocuments from Dawsonera? Broken out by FTE Enrollment

FTE Enrollment	Mean	Median	Minimum	Maximum
less than 3000	0,00	0,00	0,00	0,00
3000 - 7000	90,91	0,00	0,00	1000,00
more than 7000	0,00	0,00	0,00	0,00

Table 6.5.4 How much did your library spend ($) in the past year on eBooks or eDocuments from Dawsonera? Broken out by Annual Tuition Level

Annual Tuition Level	Mean	Median	Minimum	Maximum
less than $6000	0,00	0,00	0,00	0,00
$6000 - $20000	90,91	0,00	0,00	1000,00
more than $20000	0,00	0,00	0,00	0,00

Table 6.5.5 How much did your library spend ($) in the past year on eBooks or eDocuments from Dawsonera? Broken out by Carnegie Class

Carnegie Class	Mean	Median	Minimum	Maximum
Community College / 4-Year College	0,00	0,00	0,00	0,00
MA/PHD Granting / Research University	71,43	0,00	0,00	1000,00

Table 6.6.1 How much did your library spend ($) in the past year on eBooks or eDocuments from Knovel?

	Mean	Median	Minimum	Maximum
Entire sample	1089,29	0,00	0,00	25000,00

Table 6.6.2 How much did your library spend ($) in the past year on eBooks or eDocuments from Knovel? Broken out by College Type

College Type	Mean	Median	Minimum	Maximum
Public	0,00	0,00	0,00	0,00
Private	3812,50	0,00	0,00	25000,00

Table 6.6.3 How much did your library spend ($) in the past year on eBooks or eDocuments from Knovel? Broken out by FTE Enrollment

FTE Enrollment	Mean	Median	Minimum	Maximum
less than 3000	0,00	0,00	0,00	0,00
3000 - 7000	0,00	0,00	0,00	0,00
more than 7000	3050,00	0,00	0,00	25000,00

Table 6.6.4 How much did your library spend ($) in the past year on eBooks or eDocuments from Knovel? Broken out by Annual Tuition Level

Annual Tuition Level	Mean	Median	Minimum	Maximum
less than $6000	0,00	0,00	0,00	0,00
$6000 - $20000	0,00	0,00	0,00	0,00
more than $20000	4357,14	0,00	0,00	25000,00

Table 6.6.5 How much did your library spend ($) in the past year on eBooks or eDocuments from Knovel? Broken out by Carnegie Class

Carnegie Class	Mean	Median	Minimum	Maximum
Community College / 4-Year College	0,00	0,00	0,00	0,00
MA/PHD Granting / Research University	2346,15	0,00	0,00	25000,00

Table 6.7.1 How much did your library spend ($) in the past year on eBooks or eDocuments from EBSCO/NetLibrary?

	Mean	Median	Minimum	Maximum
Entire sample	7731,91	1888,00	0,00	125000,00

Table 6.7.2 How much did your library spend ($) in the past year on eBooks or eDocuments from EBSCO/NetLibrary? Broken out by College Type

College Type	Mean	Median	Minimum	Maximum
Public	9225,00	650,00	0,00	125000,00
Private	4447,12	2558,50	0,00	15000,00

Table 6.7.3 How much did your library spend ($) in the past year on eBooks or eDocuments from EBSCO/NetLibrary? Broken out by FTE Enrollment

FTE Enrollment	Mean	Median	Minimum	Maximum
less than 3000	1417,55	0,00	0,00	5000,00
3000 - 7000	6045,45	4000,00	0,00	15000,00
more than 7000	16532,82	1700,00	0,00	125000,00

Table 6.7.4 How much did your library spend ($) in the past year on eBooks or eDocuments from EBSCO/NetLibrary? Broken out by Annual Tuition Level

Annual Tuition Level	Mean	Median	Minimum	Maximum
less than $6000	14400,00	3750,00	0,00	125000,00
$6000 - $20000	2740,91	0,00	0,00	15000,00
more than $20000	4941,24	2717,00	500,00	15000,00

Table 6.7.5 How much did your library spend ($) in the past year on eBooks or eDocuments from EBSCO/NetLibrary? Broken out by Carnegie Class

Carnegie Class	Mean	Median	Minimum	Maximum
Community College / 4-Year College	3294,81	1858,50	0,00	13000,00
MA/PHD Granting / Research University	12169,01	1888,00	0,00	125000,00

Table 6.8.1 How much did your library spend ($) in the past year on eBooks or eDocuments from Baker&Taylor?

	Mean	Median	Minimum	Maximum
Entire sample	3519,13	0,00	0,00	50000,00

Table 6.8.2 How much did your library spend ($) in the past year on eBooks or eDocuments from Baker&Taylor? Broken out by College Type

College Type	Mean	Median	Minimum	Maximum
Public	3026,09	0,00	0,00	50000,00
Private	4875,00	0,00	0,00	39000,00

Table 6.8.3 How much did your library spend ($) in the past year on eBooks or eDocuments from Baker&Taylor? Broken out by FTE Enrollment

FTE Enrollment	Mean	Median	Minimum	Maximum
less than 3000	0,00	0,00	0,00	0,00
3000 - 7000	4136,36	0,00	0,00	39000,00
more than 7000	5461,27	0,00	0,00	50000,00

Table 6.8.4 How much did your library spend ($) in the past year on eBooks or eDocuments from Baker&Taylor? Broken out by Annual Tuition Level

Annual Tuition Level	Mean	Median	Minimum	Maximum
less than $6000	5136,36	0,00	0,00	50000,00
$6000 - $20000	839,50	0,00	0,00	5000,00
more than $20000	5571,43	0,00	0,00	39000,00

Table 6.8.5 How much did your library spend ($) in the past year on eBooks or eDocuments from Baker&Taylor? Broken out by Carnegie Class

Carnegie Class	Mean	Median	Minimum	Maximum
Community College / 4-Year College	3033,33	0,00	0,00	39000,00
MA/PHD Granting / Research University	4004,93	0,00	0,00	50000,00

Table 6.9.1 How much did your library spend ($) in the past year on eBooks or eDocuments from Blackwell?

	Mean	Median	Minimum	Maximum
Entire sample	8,62	0,00	0,00	250,00

Table 6.9.2 How much did your library spend ($) in the past year on eBooks or eDocuments from Blackwell? Broken out by College Type

College Type	Mean	Median	Minimum	Maximum
Public	0,00	0,00	0,00	0,00
Private	31,25	0,00	0,00	250,00

Table 6.9.3 How much did your library spend ($) in the past year on eBooks or eDocuments from Blackwell? Broken out by FTE Enrollment

FTE Enrollment	Mean	Median	Minimum	Maximum
less than 3000	0,00	0,00	0,00	0,00
3000 - 7000	22,73	0,00	0,00	250,00
more than 7000	0,00	0,00	0,00	0,00

Table 6.9.4 How much did your library spend ($) in the past year on eBooks or eDocuments from Blackwell? Broken out by Annual Tuition Level

Annual Tuition Level	Mean	Median	Minimum	Maximum
less than $6000	0,00	0,00	0,00	0,00
$6000 - $20000	0,00	0,00	0,00	0,00
more than $20000	35,71	0,00	0,00	250,00

Table 6.9.5 How much did your library spend ($) in the past year on eBooks or eDocuments from Blackwell? Broken out by Carnegie Class

Carnegie Class	Mean	Median	Minimum	Maximum
Community College / 4-Year College	16,67	0,00	0,00	250,00
MA/PHD Granting / Research University	0,00	0,00	0,00	0,00

Table 6.10.1 How much did your library spend ($) in the past year on eBooks or eDocuments from Swets?

	Mean	Median	Minimum	Maximum
Entire sample	0,00	0,00	0,00	0,00

Table 6.11.1 How much did your library spend ($) in the past year on eBooks or eDocuments from EBL?

	Mean	Median	Minimum	Maximum
Entire sample	10146,55	0,00	0,00	250000,00

Table 6.11.2 How much did your library spend ($) in the past year on eBooks or eDocuments from EBL? Broken out by College Type

College Type	Mean	Median	Minimum	Maximum
Public	1226,19	0,00	0,00	10000,00
Private	33562,50	0,00	0,00	250000,00

Table 6.11.3 How much did your library spend ($) in the past year on eBooks or eDocuments from EBL? Broken out by FTE Enrollment

FTE Enrollment	Mean	Median	Minimum	Maximum
less than 3000	0,00	0,00	0,00	0,00
3000 - 7000	1886,36	0,00	0,00	10000,00
more than 7000	27350,00	0,00	0,00	250000,00

Table 6.11.4 How much did your library spend ($) in the past year on eBooks or eDocuments from EBL? Broken out by Annual Tuition Level

Annual Tuition Level	Mean	Median	Minimum	Maximum
less than $6000	977,27	0,00	0,00	10000,00
$6000 - $20000	1363,64	0,00	0,00	10000,00
more than $20000	38357,14	0,00	0,00	250000,00

Table 6.11.5 How much did your library spend ($) in the past year on eBooks or eDocuments from EBL? Broken out by Carnegie Class

Carnegie Class	Mean	Median	Minimum	Maximum
Community College / 4-Year College	716,67	0,00	0,00	10000,00
MA/PHD Granting / Research University	20250,00	0,00	0,00	250000,00

Table 6.12.1 How much did your library spend ($) in the past year on eBooks or eDocuments from Ingram/Coutts/MyiLibrary?

	Mean	Median	Minimum	Maximum
Entire sample	551,72	0,00	0,00	10000,00

Table 6.12.2 How much did your library spend ($) in the past year on eBooks or eDocuments from Ingram/Coutts/MyiLibrary? Broken out by College Type

College Type	Mean	Median	Minimum	Maximum
Public	738,10	0,00	0,00	10000,00
Private	62,50	0,00	0,00	500,00

Table 6.12.3 How much did your library spend ($) in the past year on eBooks or eDocuments from Ingram/Coutts/MyiLibrary? Broken out by FTE Enrollment

FTE Enrollment	Mean	Median	Minimum	Maximum
less than 3000	625,00	0,00	0,00	5000,00
3000 - 7000	45,45	0,00	0,00	500,00
more than 7000	1050,00	0,00	0,00	10000,00

Table 6.12.4 How much did your library spend ($) in the past year on eBooks or eDocuments from Ingram/Coutts/MyiLibrary? Broken out by Annual Tuition Level

Annual Tuition Level	Mean	Median	Minimum	Maximum
less than $6000	45,45	0,00	0,00	500,00
$6000 - $20000	1363,64	0,00	0,00	10000,00
more than $20000	71,43	0,00	0,00	500,00

Table 6.12.5 How much did your library spend ($) in the past year on eBooks or eDocuments from Ingram/Coutts/MyiLibrary? Broken out by Carnegie Class

Carnegie Class	Mean	Median	Minimum	Maximum
Community College / 4-Year College	1033,33	0,00	0,00	10000,00
MA/PHD Granting / Research University	35,71	0,00	0,00	500,00

Table 6.13.1 How much did your library spend ($) in the past year on eBooks or eDocuments from Barnes & Noble?

	Mean	Median	Minimum	Maximum
Entire sample	107,14	0,00	0,00	3000,00

Table 6.13.2 How much did your library spend ($) in the past year on eBooks or eDocuments from Barnes & Noble? Broken out by College Type

College Type	Mean	Median	Minimum	Maximum
Public	0,00	0,00	0,00	0,00
Private	375,00	0,00	0,00	3000,00

Table 6.13.3 How much did your library spend ($) in the past year on eBooks or eDocuments from Barnes & Noble? Broken out by FTE Enrollment

FTE Enrollment	Mean	Median	Minimum	Maximum
less than 3000	0,00	0,00	0,00	0,00
3000 - 7000	272,73	0,00	0,00	3000,00
more than 7000	0,00	0,00	0,00	0,00

Table 6.13.4 How much did your library spend ($) in the past year on eBooks or eDocuments from Barnes & Noble? Broken out by Annual Tuition Level

Annual Tuition Level	Mean	Median	Minimum	Maximum
less than $6000	0,00	0,00	0,00	0,00
$6000 - $20000	0,00	0,00	0,00	0,00
more than $20000	428,57	0,00	0,00	3000,00

Table 6.13.5 How much did your library spend ($) in the past year on eBooks or eDocuments from Barnes & Noble? Broken out by Carnegie Class

Carnegie Class	Mean	Median	Minimum	Maximum
Community College / 4-Year College	214,29	0,00	0,00	3000,00
MA/PHD Granting / Research University	0,00	0,00	0,00	0,00

Table 6.14.1 How much did your library spend ($) in the past year on eBooks or eDocuments from Google?

	Mean	Median	Minimum	Maximum
Entire sample	0,00	0,00	0,00	0,00

Table 6.15.1 How much did your library spend ($) in the past year on eBooks or eDocuments from All academic presses?

	Mean	Median	Minimum	Maximum
Entire sample	32107,96	0,00	0,00	742937,00

Table 6.15.2 How much did your library spend ($) in the past year on eBooks or eDocuments from All academic presses? Broken out by College Type

College Type	Mean	Median	Minimum	Maximum
Public	4995,00	0,00	0,00	80000,00
Private	99890,38	6500,00	0,00	742937,00

Table 6.15.3 How much did your library spend ($) in the past year on eBooks or eDocuments from All academic presses? Broken out by FTE Enrollment

FTE Enrollment	Mean	Median	Minimum	Maximum
less than 3000	4568,60	0,00	0,00	33186,00
3000 - 7000	1444,44	0,00	0,00	10000,00
more than 7000	93370,78	200,00	0,00	742937,00

Table 6.15.4 How much did your library spend ($) in the past year on eBooks or eDocuments from All academic presses? Broken out by Annual Tuition Level

Annual Tuition Level	Mean	Median	Minimum	Maximum
less than $6000	9188,89	0,00	0,00	80000,00
$6000 - $20000	1433,33	0,00	0,00	10000,00
more than $20000	114160,43	10000,00	0,00	742937,00

Table 6.15.5 How much did your library spend ($) in the past year on eBooks or eDocuments from All academic presses? Broken out by Carnegie Class

Carnegie Class	Mean	Median	Minimum	Maximum
Community College / 4-Year College	1192,31	0,00	0,00	10000,00
MA/PHD Granting / Research University	58901,53	0,00	0,00	742937,00

Does your library promote the use of any of the following to your library patrons (Internet Library, Project Gutenberg, HathiTrust,) and how

1) No
2) No
3) Yes, some are in the catalog. Some are in LibGuides, etc. Don't know the usage.
4) No
5) No
6) yes. not used extensively but is listed along with other paid eBook websites.
7) Yes. We don't have usage statistics.
8) The library does not promote any of: Internet Library, Project Gutenberg; The library is negotiating to join: HathiTrust
9) We have a LibGuide that lists free e-resources, but they do not get used often
10) We promote public domain materials and some are discoverable in our catalog but the use is low because of the age of most of the materials.
11) No
12) No
13) No.
14) HathiTrust, project Gutenberg. Use is only so so. We do not have all Hathi content due to copyright restrictions.
15) Only on a case-by-case basis at the reference desk. No broad promotion of eBooks has taken place in the past 5 years.
16) They are available on a=our website but not actively promoted
17) HathiTrust. Not extensive use.
18) No
19) We have links from our catalog, but that's it
20) HathiTrust Minimal use
21) yes via our database page
22) no, unknown
23) We provide marc records and links to hundreds of project Gutenberg books.
24) Useful items have catalogs in our database.
25) We have links to these resources on LibGuides; and, when a patron is looking for an eBook version of a book in the public domain we will often direct them to one of these resources.
26) On our website's eBook page
27) Promote Internet Library in selected 200-level classes and usage is minimal if that
28) N0
29) We promote them as part of the resources available. We have a website that identifies these as options
30) We provide access, but as far as I know do not promote them. That is a good idea.
31) Our Library includes all of the listed resources (Internet Library, Project Gutenberg, HathiTrust) to users, but at least following what metrics we can, use of these resources is highly limited.

32) We include the HathiTrust e-books in our Summon index. We have links to Project Gutenberg and the Internet Library on the library site, but I don't know how often they are used.

33) We use all of them. We value free resources.

34) yes, via Libguides and info literacy instruction sessions

35) We have an eBook LibGuide that lists eBook sources including the three mentioned above.

When you look to purchase an eBook how do you go about doing it? Which sources do you consult to check on eBook availability?

1) N/A
2) We only purchase EBSCO eBook collections at this time
3) Usually check EBSCO first. Librarians negotiate deals with other vendors occasionally.
4) listservs, Google
5) None. We just have ebrary and Net books and we promote whatever they offer.
6) Search YBP Gobi initially, then EBSCO/ebrary/EBL, and if still not available then seek out the publisher directly.
7) Publisher site.
8) Determine number of users and aggregator availability using YBP's Gobi3 database. Is a licence is in place? Does the licence permit the number of desired users? Place the order.
9) Check Gale's website to determine if a print reference title is available as an eBook Baker & Taylor's YBP is also checked, but we do not order non-reference titles as eBook at this time
10) Either search Oasis or EBSCO and compare prices and availability
11) Look at what is available that students and faculty would use. Talk to faculty, Buy as much as we can afford.
12) we are starting to use PDA for all purchasing
13) N/A.
14) It depends, we tend not to buy title by title. Generally we want unlimited user access and no DRM
15) We are glad to find institutional eBooks available for purchase from YBP, and occasionally find good support for academic institutions from other publishers.
16) Catalog is reviewed; vendor is approached next
17) DawsonEra - depends on course size, cost benefit of purchasing the eBook rather than multiple physical copies.
18) Coutts database
19) We don't do eBooks much - our students don't use them much
20) We use our distributor and vendor interfaces for one off purchases. Packages are generally offered by vendors and then evaluated for relevancy and usability.
21) is it available from our vendor
22) We use YBP/Gobi, compare print cost to eBook - willing to buy eBooks up to $50 more than print or up to 50 higher cost but not more than that unless needed for online/distance program
23) YBP-GOBI
24) check vendor sites for availability, moving to another paper book platform for cross-availability review
25) We primarily purchase packages, many through consortia agreements

26) Generally, we start by checking availability with our two major suppliers, ebrary and EBSCO. If the eBook is not available from them, we then check the publisher's website for eBook availability.

27) YBP or EBSCO

28) Do not purchase eBooks only have NetLibrary and ebrary

29) Don't buy individual eBooks- too expensive. We get subscriptions

30) YBP is our jobber. We select through them with EBSCO, ebrary, and publisher in that order of preference for the system the e-book is available.

31) With our book jobber/vendor or publisher direct to see what restrictions (if any) come with the book.

32) Generally, we do not look to purchase e-books title by title as yet; we purchase normally by collections, either by subject collections or by publisher. The most cost-effective deals are only available this way. Many of the titles available only for purchase as individual titles are expensive & detract from the whole advantage of the electronic format. Consequently many of these titles are simply more sensibly bought as physical copies.

33) Our default is to add e-books to the patron-driven acquisition profile on ebrary if there's a specific title we want. If it's not available that way, we'll look into a title purchase through YBP/GOBI with one of our vendors. If we can't get the e-book that way, we're not likely to get it. We wouldn't add a subscription/collection for just one e-book. The whole set would have to be of value.

34) We don't purchase individual items yet. We buy them in databases.

35) we check publishers and distributors

36) ebrary, EBSCO, Safari, Books 24x7

CHAPTER 3 – eBook Formats

Table 7.1 Approximately what percentage of the eBook titles your library offers are in PDF format?

	Mean	Median	Minimum	Maximum
Entire sample	68,83	80,00	0,00	100,00

Table 7.2 Approximately what percentage of the eBook titles your library offers are in PDF format? Broken out by College Type

College Type	Mean	Median	Minimum	Maximum
Public	74,81	85,00	0,00	100,00
Private	54,89	60,00	0,00	100,00

Table 7.3 Approximately what percentage of the eBook titles your library offers are in PDF format? Broken out by FTE Enrollment

FTE Enrollment	Mean	Median	Minimum	Maximum
less than 3000	53,63	70,00	0,00	100,00
3000 - 7000	85,45	85,00	60,00	100,00
more than 7000	63,27	75,00	2,00	100,00

Table 7.4 Approximately what percentage of the eBook titles your library offers are in PDF format? Broken out by Annual Tuition Level

Annual Tuition Level	Mean	Median	Minimum	Maximum
less than $6000	79,67	85,00	2,00	100,00
$6000 - $20000	62,83	67,50	0,00	100,00
more than $20000	66,00	80,00	0,00	100,00

Table 7.5 Approximately what percentage of the eBook titles your library offers are in PDF format? Broken out by Carnegie Class

Carnegie Class	Mean	Median	Minimum	Maximum
Community College / 4-Year College	72,79	80,00	0,00	100,00
MA/PHD Granting / Research University	65,38	82,50	0,00	100,00

CHAPTER 4 – eBook Distribution

Table 8 What percentage of the library's total spending ($) on eBooks was with the following type of vendor: Aggregators, Individual Publishers?

For example Amazon or NetLibrary would be considered aggregators while John Wiley & Sons would be an individual publisher?

Table 8.1.1 What percentage of the library's total spending ($) on eBooks was with Aggregators?

	Mean	Median	Minimum	Maximum
Entire sample	78,21	90,00	0,00	100,00

Table 8.1.2 What percentage of the library's total spending ($) on eBooks was with Aggregators? Broken out by College Type

College Type	Mean	Median	Minimum	Maximum
Public	80,70	90,00	0,00	100,00
Private	72,50	74,50	21,00	100,00

Table 8.1.3 What percentage of the library's total spending ($) on eBooks was with Aggregators? Broken out by FTE Enrollment

FTE Enrollment	Mean	Median	Minimum	Maximum
less than 3000	74,64	100,00	0,00	100,00
3000 - 7000	82,17	95,00	1,00	100,00
more than 7000	77,40	85,00	30,00	95,00

Table 8.1.4 What percentage of the library's total spending ($) on eBooks was with Aggregators? Broken out by Annual Tuition Level

Annual Tuition Level	Mean	Median	Minimum	Maximum
less than $6000	92,08	95,00	70,00	100,00
$6000 - $20000	65,10	77,50	0,00	100,00
more than $20000	75,00	79,00	21,00	100,00

Table 8.1.5 What percentage of the library's total spending ($) on eBooks was with Aggregators? Broken out by Carnegie Class

Carnegie Class	Mean	Median	Minimum	Maximum
Community College / 4-Year College	84,06	95,00	0,00	100,00
MA/PHD Granting / Research University	72,71	80,00	1,00	100,00

Table 8.2.1 What percentage of the library's total spending ($) on eBooks was with Individual Publishers?

	Mean	Median	Minimum	Maximum
Entire sample	18,45	10,00	0,00	99,00

Table 8.2. What percentage of the library's total spending ($) on eBooks was with Individual Publishers? Broken out by College Type

College Type	Mean	Median	Minimum	Maximum
Public	14,96	10,00	0,00	99,00
Private	26,50	20,50	0,00	79,00

Table 8.2.3 What percentage of the library's total spending ($) on eBooks was with Individual Publishers? Broken out by FTE Enrollment

FTE Enrollment	Mean	Median	Minimum	Maximum
less than 3000	16,27	0,00	0,00	79,00
3000 - 7000	17,00	5,00	0,00	99,00
more than 7000	22,60	15,00	5,00	70,00

Table 8.2.4 What percentage of the library's total spending ($) on eBooks was with Individual Publishers? Broken out by Annual Tuition Level

Annual Tuition Level	Mean	Median	Minimum	Maximum
less than $6000	7,92	5,00	0,00	30,00
$6000 - $20000	24,90	10,00	0,00	99,00
more than $20000	24,09	20,00	0,00	79,00

Table 8.2.5 What percentage of the library's total spending ($) on eBooks was with Individual Publishers? Broken out by Carnegie Class

Carnegie Class	Mean	Median	Minimum	Maximum
Community College / 4-Year College	9,06	0,00	0,00	50,00
MA/PHD Granting / Research University	27,29	20,00	0,00	99,00

Table 9 What percentage of the library's total eBook ordering was made through the following channels:

(We are asking who did you order from and pay the bill to)

Table 9.1.1 What percentage of the library's total eBook ordering was made through eBook divisions of a traditional book jobber or book distributor such as EBSCO's NetLibrary, Ingram's MyiLibrary or Baker & Taylor's eBook Library and other such divisions?

	Mean	Median	Minimum	Maximum
Entire sample	48,53	50,00	0,00	100,00

Table 9.1.2 What percentage of the library's total eBook ordering was made through eBook divisions of a traditional book jobber or book distributor such as EBSCO's NetLibrary, Ingram's MyiLibrary or Baker & Taylor's eBook Library and other such divisions? Broken out by College Type

College Type	Mean	Median	Minimum	Maximum
Public	52,29	75,00	0,00	100,00
Private	39,50	30,00	0,00	100,00

Table 9.1.3 What percentage of the library's total eBook ordering was made through eBook divisions of a traditional book jobber or book distributor such as EBSCO's NetLibrary, Ingram's MyiLibrary or Baker & Taylor's eBook Library and other such divisions? Broken out by FTE Enrollment

FTE Enrollment	Mean	Median	Minimum	Maximum
less than 3000	21,82	0,00	0,00	100,00
3000 - 7000	70,83	87,50	0,00	100,00
more than 7000	50,91	50,00	0,00	100,00

Table 9.1.4 What percentage of the library's total eBook ordering was made through eBook divisions of a traditional book jobber or book distributor such as EBSCO's NetLibrary, Ingram's MyiLibrary or Baker & Taylor's eBook Library and other such divisions? Broken out by Annual Tuition Level

Annual Tuition Level	Mean	Median	Minimum	Maximum
less than $6000	46,67	50,00	0,00	100,00
$6000 - $20000	54,09	65,00	0,00	100,00
more than $20000	45,00	40,00	0,00	100,00

Table 9.1.5 What percentage of the library's total eBook ordering was made through eBook divisions of a traditional book jobber or book distributor such as EBSCO's NetLibrary, Ingram's MyiLibrary or Baker & Taylor's eBook Library and other such divisions? Broken out by Carnegie Class

Carnegie Class	Mean	Median	Minimum	Maximum
Community College / 4-Year College	43,82	20,00	0,00	100,00
MA/PHD Granting / Research University	53,24	50,00	0,00	100,00

Table 9.2.1 What percentage of the library's total eBook ordering was made through an electronic information aggregator not connected to a major book jobber or distributor?

	Mean	Median	Minimum	Maximum
Entire sample	30,32	7,50	0,00	100,00

Table 9.2.2 What percentage of the library's total eBook ordering was made through an electronic information aggregator not connected to a major book jobber or distributor? Broken out by College Type

College Type	Mean	Median	Minimum	Maximum
Public	27,29	0,00	0,00	100,00
Private	37,60	35,00	0,00	100,00

Table 9.2.3 What percentage of the library's total eBook ordering was made through an electronic information aggregator not connected to a major book jobber or distributor? Broken out by FTE Enrollment

FTE Enrollment	Mean	Median	Minimum	Maximum
less than 3000	47,36	50,00	0,00	100,00
3000 - 7000	14,17	0,00	0,00	100,00
more than 7000	30,91	20,00	0,00	90,00

Table 9.2.4 What percentage of the library's total eBook ordering was made through an electronic information aggregator not connected to a major book jobber or distributor? Broken out by Annual Tuition Level

Annual Tuition Level	Mean	Median	Minimum	Maximum
less than $6000	40,00	5,00	0,00	100,00
$6000 - $20000	15,91	0,00	0,00	90,00
more than $20000	34,18	25,00	0,00	100,00

Table 9.2. What percentage of the library's total eBook ordering was made through an electronic information aggregator not connected to a major book jobber or distributor? Broken out by Carnegie Class

Carnegie Class	Mean	Median	Minimum	Maximum
Community College / 4-Year College	36,18	5,00	0,00	100,00
MA/PHD Granting / Research University	24,47	10,00	0,00	90,00

Table 9.3.1 What percentage of the library's total eBook ordering was made direct from a publisher?

	Mean	Median	Minimum	Maximum
Entire sample	14,65	5,00	0,00	99,00

Table 9.3.2 What percentage of the library's total eBook ordering was made direct from a publisher? Broken out by College Type

College Type	Mean	Median	Minimum	Maximum
Public	11,42	5,00	0,00	99,00
Private	22,40	20,00	0,00	70,00

Table 9.3.3 What percentage of the library's total eBook ordering was made direct from a publisher? Broken out by FTE Enrollment

FTE Enrollment	Mean	Median	Minimum	Maximum
less than 3000	12,64	0,00	0,00	50,00
3000 - 7000	14,92	2,50	0,00	99,00
more than 7000	16,36	10,00	0,00	70,00

Table 9.3.4 What percentage of the library's total eBook ordering was made direct from a publisher? Broken out by Annual Tuition Level

Annual Tuition Level	Mean	Median	Minimum	Maximum
less than $6000	5,00	2,50	0,00	15,00
$6000 - $20000	19,45	10,00	0,00	99,00
more than $20000	20,36	20,00	0,00	70,00

Table 9.3.5 What percentage of the library's total eBook ordering was made direct from a publisher? Broken out by Carnegie Class

Carnegie Class	Mean	Median	Minimum	Maximum
Community College / 4-Year College	8,24	0,00	0,00	50,00
MA/PHD Granting / Research University	21,06	10,00	0,00	99,00

Table 10.1 What percentage of the library's eBook collection spending is through contracts negotiated by a consortium?

	Mean	Median	Minimum	Maximum
Entire sample	30,69	20,00	0,00	100,00

Table 10.2 What percentage of the library's eBook collection spending is through contracts negotiated by a consortium? Broken out by College Type

College Type	Mean	Median	Minimum	Maximum
Public	27,29	10,00	0,00	100,00
Private	38,09	21,00	0,00	100,00

Table 10.3 What percentage of the library's eBook collection spending is through contracts negotiated by a consortium? Broken out by FTE Enrollment

FTE Enrollment	Mean	Median	Minimum	Maximum
less than 3000	40,92	23,00	0,00	100,00
3000 - 7000	22,50	10,00	0,00	75,00
more than 7000	28,45	5,00	0,00	100,00

Table 10.4 What percentage of the library's eBook collection spending is through contracts negotiated by a consortium? Broken out by Annual Tuition Level

Annual Tuition Level	Mean	Median	Minimum	Maximum
less than $6000	23,75	15,00	0,00	100,00
$6000 - $20000	39,17	32,50	0,00	100,00
more than $20000	29,00	20,00	0,00	100,00

Table 10.5 What percentage of the library's eBook collection spending is through contracts negotiated by a consortium? Broken out by Carnegie Class

Carnegie Class	Mean	Median	Minimum	Maximum
Community College / 4-Year College	31,76	25,00	0,00	100,00
MA/PHD Granting / Research University	29,67	17,50	0,00	100,00

CHAPTER 5 – eBook Circulation Figures

Table 11.1 What has been the growth rate of eBook use at your library in the past year, comparing if you can the last three months with the same period last year?

	Mean	Median	Minimum	Maximum
Entire sample	69,38	15,00	-57,00	900,00

Table 11.2 What has been the growth rate of eBook use at your library in the past year, comparing if you can the last three months with the same period last year? Broken out by College Type

College Type	Mean	Median	Minimum	Maximum
Public	101,47	15,00	-50,00	900,00
Private	15,89	15,00	-57,00	50,00

Table 11.3 What has been the growth rate of eBook use at your library in the past year, comparing if you can the last three months with the same period last year? Broken out by FTE Enrollment

FTE Enrollment	Mean	Median	Minimum	Maximum
less than 3000	114,71	0,00	-57,00	900,00
3000 - 7000	34,29	15,00	5,00	120,00
more than 7000	62,20	25,00	-3,00	250,00

Table 11.4 What has been the growth rate of eBook use at your library in the past year, comparing if you can the last three months with the same period last year? Broken out by Annual Tuition Level

Annual Tuition Level	Mean	Median	Minimum	Maximum
less than $6000	14,50	5,00	-50,00	120,00
$6000 - $20000	143,50	20,00	0,00	900,00
more than $20000	17,88	22,50	-57,00	50,00

Table 11.5 What has been the growth rate of eBook use at your library in the past year, comparing if you can the last three months with the same period last year? Broken out by Carnegie Class

Carnegie Class	Mean	Median	Minimum	Maximum
Community College / 4-Year College	94,50	10,00	-50,00	900,00
MA/PHD Granting / Research University	51,43	22,50	-57,00	250,00

CHAPTER 6 – Purchasing Models

Table 12 What percentage of your library's eBook spending is accounted for by the following types of model?

Table 12.1.1 What percentage of your library's eBook spending is accounted for by a model that provides a limited number of borrowings or circulations to patrons for a specified price

	Mean	Median	Minimum	Maximum
Entire sample	26,24	0,00	0,00	100,00

Table 12.1.2 What percentage of your library's eBook spending is accounted for by a model that provides a limited number of borrowings or circulations to patrons for a specified price Broken out by College Type

College Type	Mean	Median	Minimum	Maximum
Public	26,70	0,00	0,00	100,00
Private	25,20	1,00	0,00	95,00

Table 12.1.3 What percentage of your library's eBook spending is accounted for by a model that provides a limited number of borrowings or circulations to patrons for a specified price Broken out by FTE Enrollment

FTE Enrollment	Mean	Median	Minimum	Maximum
less than 3000	16,36	0,00	0,00	70,00
3000 - 7000	38,18	15,00	0,00	100,00
more than 7000	24,18	10,00	0,00	100,00

Table 12.1.4 What percentage of your library's eBook spending is accounted for by a model that provides a limited number of borrowings or circulations to patrons for a specified price Broken out by Annual Tuition Level

Annual Tuition Level	Mean	Median	Minimum	Maximum
less than $6000	14,17	0,00	0,00	85,00
$6000 - $20000	34,40	15,00	0,00	100,00
more than $20000	32,00	2,00	0,00	100,00

Table 12.1.5 What percentage of your library's eBook spending is accounted for by a model that provides a limited number of borrowings or circulations to patrons for a specified price Broken out by Carnegie Class

Carnegie Class	Mean	Median	Minimum	Maximum
Community College / 4-Year College	22,35	0,00	0,00	100,00
MA/PHD Granting / Research University	30,38	11,00	0,00	100,00

Table 12.2.1 What percentage of your library's eBook spending is accounted for by subscriptions for unlimited patron use for a specified period of time

	Mean	Median	Minimum	Maximum
Entire sample	40,09	30,00	0,00	100,00

Table 12.2.2 What percentage of your library's eBook spending is accounted for by subscriptions for unlimited patron use for a specified period of time Broken out by College Type

College Type	Mean	Median	Minimum	Maximum
Public	39,70	30,00	0,00	100,00
Private	41,00	27,50	0,00	100,00

Table 12.2.3 What percentage of your library's eBook spending is accounted for by subscriptions for unlimited patron use for a specified period of time Broken out by FTE Enrollment

FTE Enrollment	Mean	Median	Minimum	Maximum
less than 3000	50,91	30,00	0,00	100,00
3000 - 7000	41,82	40,00	0,00	100,00
more than 7000	27,55	25,00	0,00	75,00

Table 12.2.4 What percentage of your library's eBook spending is accounted for by subscriptions for unlimited patron use for a specified period of time Broken out by Annual Tuition Level

Annual Tuition Level	Mean	Median	Minimum	Maximum
less than $6000	54,58	52,50	0,00	100,00
$6000 - $20000	25,80	15,00	0,00	95,00
more than $20000	37,27	25,00	0,00	100,00

Table 12.2.5 What percentage of your library's eBook spending is accounted for by subscriptions for unlimited patron use for a specified period of time Broken out by Carnegie Class

Carnegie Class	Mean	Median	Minimum	Maximum
Community College / 4-Year College	53,53	65,00	0,00	100,00
MA/PHD Granting / Research University	25,81	22,50	0,00	90,00

Table 12.3.1 What percentage of your library's eBook spending is accounted for by an ownership model similar to print purchases of books where the library becomes the perpetual owner of the book as long as it is used only by recognized library patrons

	Mean	Median	Minimum	Maximum
Entire sample	28,58	20,00	0,00	100,00

Table 12.3.2 What percentage of your library's eBook spending is accounted for by an ownership model similar to print purchases of books where the library becomes the perpetual owner of the book as long as it is used only by recognized library patrons Broken out by College Type

College Type	Mean	Median	Minimum	Maximum
Public	27,96	15,00	0,00	100,00
Private	30,00	22,50	0,00	75,00

Table 12.3.3 What percentage of your library's eBook spending is accounted for by an ownership model similar to print purchases of books where the library becomes the perpetual owner of the book as long as it is used only by recognized library patrons Broken out by FTE Enrollment

FTE Enrollment	Mean	Median	Minimum	Maximum
less than 3000	23,64	5,00	0,00	100,00
3000 - 7000	18,64	10,00	0,00	75,00
more than 7000	43,45	40,00	0,00	80,00

Table 12.3.4 What percentage of your library's eBook spending is accounted for by an ownership model similar to print purchases of books where the library becomes the perpetual owner of the book as long as it is used only by recognized library patrons Broken out by Annual Tuition Level

Annual Tuition Level	Mean	Median	Minimum	Maximum
less than $6000	28,75	15,00	0,00	100,00
$6000 - $20000	29,80	17,50	0,00	100,00
more than $20000	27,27	20,00	0,00	75,00

Table 12.3.5 What percentage of your library's eBook spending is accounted for by an ownership model similar to print purchases of books where the library becomes the perpetual owner of the book as long as it is used only by recognized library patrons Broken out by Carnegie Class

Carnegie Class	Mean	Median	Minimum	Maximum
Community College / 4-Year College	17,35	5,00	0,00	100,00
MA/PHD Granting / Research University	40,50	36,50	0,00	100,00

Table 12.4. What percentage of your library's eBook spending is accounted for by a pay per individual use where the library pays for each individual "check out" by patrons

	Mean	Median	Minimum	Maximum
Entire sample	1,76	0,00	0,00	25,00

Table 12.4.2 What percentage of your library's eBook spending is accounted for by a pay per individual use where the library pays for each individual "check out" by patrons Broken out by College Type

College Type	Mean	Median	Minimum	Maximum
Public	1,30	0,00	0,00	25,00
Private	2,80	0,00	0,00	23,00

Table 12.4.3 What percentage of your library's eBook spending is accounted for by a pay per individual use where the library pays for each individual "check out" by patrons Broken out by FTE Enrollment

FTE Enrollment	Mean	Median	Minimum	Maximum
less than 3000	0,00	0,00	0,00	0,00
3000 - 7000	0,45	0,00	0,00	5,00
more than 7000	4,82	0,00	0,00	25,00

Table 12.4.4 What percentage of your library's eBook spending is accounted for by pay per individual use where the library pays for each individual "check out" by patrons Broken out by Annual Tuition Level

Annual Tuition Level	Mean	Median	Minimum	Maximum
less than $6000	2,50	0,00	0,00	25,00
$6000 - $20000	0,00	0,00	0,00	0,00
more than $20000	2,55	0,00	0,00	23,00

Table 12.4.5 What percentage of your library's eBook spending is accounted for by pay per individual use where the library pays for each individual "check out" by patrons Broken out by Carnegie Class

Carnegie Class	Mean	Median	Minimum	Maximum
Community College / 4-Year College	0,29	0,00	0,00	5,00
MA/PHD Granting / Research University	3,31	0,00	0,00	25,00

Table 13 Over the past year what has been the change in your spending in percentage terms on each of the following models:

(these answers should be some percentage of 100%)

Table 13.1.1 Over the past year what has been the change in your spending in percentage terms on a model that provides a limited number of borrowings or circulations to patrons for a specified price?

	Mean	Median	Minimum	Maximum
Entire sample	19,57	0,00	0,00	100,00

Table 13.1.2 Over the past year what has been the change in your spending in percentage terms on a model that provides a limited number of borrowings or circulations to patrons for a specified price? Broken out by College Type

College Type	Mean	Median	Minimum	Maximum
Public	16,52	0,00	0,00	100,00
Private	26,67	0,00	0,00	70,00

Table 13.1.3 Over the past year what has been the change in your spending in percentage terms on a model that provides a limited number of borrowings or circulations to patrons for a specified price? Broken out by FTE Enrollment

FTE Enrollment	Mean	Median	Minimum	Maximum
less than 3000	22,50	0,00	0,00	70,00
3000 - 7000	19,09	0,00	0,00	100,00
more than 7000	17,91	0,00	0,00	100,00

Table 13.1.4 Over the past year what has been the change in your spending in percentage terms on a model that provides a limited number of borrowings or circulations to patrons for a specified price? Broken out by Annual Tuition Level

Annual Tuition Level	Mean	Median	Minimum	Maximum
less than $6000	5,20	0,00	0,00	50,00
$6000 - $20000	19,50	0,00	0,00	100,00
more than $20000	34,00	20,00	0,00	100,00

Table 13.1.5 Over the past year what has been the change in your spending in percentage terms on a model that provides a limited number of borrowings or circulations to patrons for a specified price? Broken out by Carnegie Class

Carnegie Class	Mean	Median	Minimum	Maximum
Community College / 4-Year College	20,00	0,00	0,00	100,00
MA/PHD Granting / Research University	19,24	0,00	0,00	100,00

Table 13.2.1 Over the past year what has been the change in your spending in percentage terms on subscriptions that allow unlimited patron use for a specified period of time?

	Mean	Median	Minimum	Maximum
Entire sample	27,42	10,00	0,00	100,00

Table 13.2.2 Over the past year what has been the change in your spending in percentage terms on a subscription for unlimited patron use for a specified period of time? Broken out by College Type

College Type	Mean	Median	Minimum	Maximum
Public	28,64	5,00	0,00	100,00
Private	24,44	20,00	0,00	90,00

Table 13.2.3 Over the past year what has been the change in your spending in percentage terms on a subscription for unlimited patron use for a specified period of time? Broken out by FTE Enrollment

FTE Enrollment	Mean	Median	Minimum	Maximum
less than 3000	40,00	25,00	0,00	100,00
3000 - 7000	35,91	20,00	0,00	100,00
more than 7000	8,64	5,00	0,00	40,00

Table 13.2.4 Over the past year what has been the change in your spending in percentage terms on a subscription for unlimited patron use for a specified period of time? Broken out by Annual Tuition Level

Annual Tuition Level	Mean	Median	Minimum	Maximum
less than $6000	38,18	5,00	0,00	100,00
$6000 - $20000	21,00	7,50	0,00	95,00
more than $20000	22,00	20,00	0,00	90,00

Table 13.2.5 Over the past year what has been the change in your spending in percentage terms on a subscription for unlimited patron use for a specified period of time? Broken out by Carnegie Class

Carnegie Class	Mean	Median	Minimum	Maximum
Community College / 4-Year College	39,29	17,50	0,00	100,00
MA/PHD Granting / Research University	17,65	5,00	0,00	90,00

Table 13.3.1 Over the past year what has been the change in your spending in percentage terms on an ownership model similar to print purchases of books where the library becomes the perpetual owner of the book as long as it is used only by recognized library patrons?

	Mean	Median	Minimum	Maximum
Entire sample	25,93	7,50	-5,00	200,00

Table 13.3.2 Over the past year what has been the change in your spending in percentage terms on an ownership model similar to print purchases of books where the library becomes the perpetual owner of the book as long as it is used only by recognized library patrons? Broken out by College Type

College Type	Mean	Median	Minimum	Maximum
Public	29,43	5,00	0,00	200,00
Private	17,78	10,00	-5,00	65,00

Table 13.3.3 Over the past year what has been the change in your spending in percentage terms on an ownership model similar to print purchases of books where the library becomes the perpetual owner of the book as long as it is used only by recognized library patrons? Broken out by FTE Enrollment

FTE Enrollment	Mean	Median	Minimum	Maximum
less than 3000	45,00	15,00	0,00	200,00
3000 - 7000	18,18	10,00	0,00	65,00
more than 7000	19,82	5,00	-5,00	98,00

Table 13.3.4 Over the past year what has been the change in your spending in percentage terms on an ownership model similar to print purchases of books where the library becomes the perpetual owner of the book as long as it is used only by recognized library patrons? Broken out by Annual Tuition Level

Annual Tuition Level	Mean	Median	Minimum	Maximum
less than $6000	24,80	7,50	0,00	100,00
$6000 - $20000	37,00	7,50	0,00	200,00
more than $20000	16,00	7,50	-5,00	65,00

Table 13.3.5 Over the past year what has been the change in your spending in percentage terms on an ownership model similar to print purchases of books where the library becomes the perpetual owner of the book as long as it is used only by recognized library patrons? Broken out by Carnegie Class

Carnegie Class	Mean	Median	Minimum	Maximum
Community College / 4-Year College	25,77	10,00	0,00	200,00
MA/PHD Granting / Research University	26,06	5,00	-5,00	100,00

Table 13.4.1 Over the past year what has been the change in your spending in percentage terms on a pay per individual use where the library pays for each individual "check out" by patrons?

	Mean	Median	Minimum	Maximum
Entire sample	2,83	0,00	0,00	40,00

Table 13.4.2 Over the past year what has been the change in your spending in percentage terms on a pay per individual use where the library pays for each individual "check out" by patrons? Broken out by College Type

College Type	Mean	Median	Minimum	Maximum
Public	0,71	0,00	0,00	15,00
Private	7,78	0,00	0,00	40,00

Table 13.4.3 Over the past year what has been the change in your spending in percentage terms on a pay per individual use where the library pays for each individual "check out" by patrons? Broken out by FTE Enrollment

FTE Enrollment	Mean	Median	Minimum	Maximum
less than 3000	0,00	0,00	0,00	0,00
3000 - 7000	2,27	0,00	0,00	25,00
more than 7000	5,45	0,00	0,00	40,00

Table 13.4.4 Over the past year what has been the change in your spending in percentage terms on a pay per individual use where the library pays for each individual "check out" by patrons? Broken out by Annual Tuition Level

Annual Tuition Level	Mean	Median	Minimum	Maximum
less than $6000	1,50	0,00	0,00	15,00
$6000 - $20000	0,00	0,00	0,00	0,00
more than $20000	7,00	0,00	0,00	40,00

Table 13.4.5 Over the past year what has been the change in your spending in percentage terms on a pay per individual use where the library pays for each individual "check out" by patrons? Broken out by Carnegie Class

Carnegie Class	Mean	Median	Minimum	Maximum
Community College / 4-Year College	0,00	0,00	0,00	0,00
MA/PHD Granting / Research University	5,00	0,00	0,00	40,00

Table 14.1 Apart from works in the public domain, how many eBook titles does the library own outright through purchases from publishers or other vendors?

(this figure would exclude annual subscriptions and eBooks subject to limits on the number of times that they can be borrowed or viewed)

	Mean	Median	Minimum	Maximum
Entire sample	77793,53	11000,00	0,00	1200000,00

Table 14.2 Apart from works in the public domain, how many eBook titles does the library own outright through purchases from publishers or other vendors? Broken out by College Type

College Type	Mean	Median	Minimum	Maximum
Public	40522,57	5000,00	0,00	200000,00
Private	173041,56	20000,00	100,00	1200000,00

Table 14.3 Apart from works in the public domain, how many eBook titles does the library own outright through purchases from publishers or other vendors? Broken out by FTE Enrollment

FTE Enrollment	Mean	Median	Minimum	Maximum
less than 3000	38137,67	20000,00	0,00	160000,00
3000 - 7000	15894,08	1800,00	0,00	80000,00
more than 7000	177765,91	106000,00	0,00	1200000,00

Table 14.4 Apart from works in the public domain, how many eBook titles does the library own outright through purchases from publishers or other vendors? Broken out by Annual Tuition Level

Annual Tuition Level	Mean	Median	Minimum	Maximum
less than $6000	24455,08	1095,00	0,00	125000,00
$6000 - $20000	52596,18	20000,00	0,00	200000,00
more than $20000	179708,22	55000,00	100,00	1200000,00

Table 14.5 Apart from works in the public domain, how many eBook titles does the library own outright through purchases from publishers or other vendors? Broken out by Carnegie Class

Carnegie Class	Mean	Median	Minimum	Maximum
Community College / 4-Year College	18517,38	550,00	0,00	160000,00
MA/PHD Granting / Research University	137069,69	52500,00	0,00	1200000,00

CHAPTER 7 – eBooks from Academic Presses

Table 15 What was (will be) the library's total spending ($) on eBooks from academic presses in the following years?

Table 15.1.1 What was (will be) the library's total spending ($) on eBooks from academic presses in 2013-14?

	Mean	Median	Minimum	Maximum
Entire sample	5425,91	70,00	0,00	45000,00

Table 15.1.2 What was (will be) the library's total spending ($) on eBooks from academic presses in 2013-14? Broken out by College Type

College Type	Mean	Median	Minimum	Maximum
Public	5752,33	55,00	0,00	45000,00
Private	4726,43	85,00	0,00	20000,00

Table 15.1.3 What was (will be) the library's total spending ($) on eBooks from academic presses in 2013-14? Broken out by FTE Enrollment

FTE Enrollment	Mean	Median	Minimum	Maximum
less than 3000	3375,00	0,00	0,00	20000,00
3000 - 7000	3256,88	1027,50	0,00	11000,00
more than 7000	11052,50	3792,50	0,00	45000,00

Table 15.1.4 What was (will be) the library's total spending ($) on eBooks from academic presses in 2013-14? Broken out by Annual Tuition Level

Annual Tuition Level	Mean	Median	Minimum	Maximum
less than $6000	6895,00	55,00	0,00	45000,00
$6000 - $20000	3461,43	30,00	0,00	13700,00
more than $20000	5514,17	1542,50	0,00	20000,00

Table 15.1.5 What was (will be) the library's total spending ($) on eBooks from academic presses in 2013-14? Broken out by Carnegie Class

Carnegie Class	Mean	Median	Minimum	Maximum
Community College / 4-Year College	2117,22	55,00	0,00	11000,00
MA/PHD Granting / Research University	7716,54	85,00	0,00	45000,00

Table 15.2.1 What was (will be) the library's total spending ($) on eBooks from academic presses in 2014-15 (anticipated)?

	Mean	Median	Minimum	Maximum
Entire sample	6449,35	30,00	0,00	65000,00

Table 15.2.2 What was (will be) the library's total spending ($) on eBooks from academic presses in 2014-15 (anticipated)? Broken out by College Type

College Type	Mean	Median	Minimum	Maximum
Public	7203,13	25,00	0,00	65000,00
Private	4726,43	85,00	0,00	20000,00

Table 15.2.3 What was (will be) the library's total spending ($) on eBooks from academic presses in 2014-15 (anticipated)? Broken out by FTE Enrollment

FTE Enrollment	Mean	Median	Minimum	Maximum
less than 3000	3277,78	0,00	0,00	20000,00
3000 - 7000	3277,50	1110,00	0,00	11000,00
more than 7000	15435,83	3792,50	0,00	65000,00

Table 15.2.4 What was (will be) the library's total spending ($) on eBooks from academic presses in 2014-15 (anticipated)? Broken out by Annual Tuition Level

Annual Tuition Level	Mean	Median	Minimum	Maximum
less than $6000	8772,00	260,00	0,00	65000,00
$6000 - $20000	3932,86	0,00	0,00	20000,00
more than $20000	5514,17	1542,50	0,00	20000,00

Table 15.2.5 What was (will be) the library's total spending ($) on eBooks from academic presses in 2014-15 (anticipated)? Broken out by Carnegie Class

Carnegie Class	Mean	Median	Minimum	Maximum
Community College / 4-Year College	1672,00	10,00	0,00	11000,00
MA/PHD Granting / Research University	10124,23	85,00	0,00	65000,00

Table 16.1 About what percentage of the books that your library desires to order from academic presses are typically available as eBooks?

	Mean	Median	Minimum	Maximum
Entire sample	28,64	20,00	0,00	75,00

Table 16.2 About what percentage of the books that your library desires to order from academic presses are typically available as eBooks? Broken out by College Type

College Type	Mean	Median	Minimum	Maximum
Public	28,75	20,00	0,00	75,00
Private	28,33	30,00	0,00	50,00

Table 16.3 About what percentage of the books that your library desires to order from academic presses are typically available as eBooks? Broken out by FTE Enrollment

FTE Enrollment	Mean	Median	Minimum	Maximum
less than 3000	15,00	0,00	0,00	75,00
3000 - 7000	20,00	15,00	0,00	40,00
more than 7000	52,14	50,00	20,00	75,00

Table 16.4 About what percentage of the books that your library desires to order from academic presses are typically available as eBooks? Broken out by Annual Tuition Level

Annual Tuition Level	Mean	Median	Minimum	Maximum
less than $6000	17,22	10,00	0,00	75,00
$6000 - $20000	43,57	40,00	0,00	75,00
more than $20000	28,33	30,00	0,00	50,00

Table 16.5 About what percentage of the books that your library desires to order from academic presses are typically available as eBooks? Broken out by Carnegie Class

Carnegie Class	Mean	Median	Minimum	Maximum
Community College / 4-Year College	20,91	10,00	0,00	75,00
MA/PHD Granting / Research University	36,36	40,00	0,00	75,00

Table 17.1 What percentage of the books that you order from academic presses do you order in an eBook format?

(including those titles that you order in both print and eBook formats)

	Mean	Median	Minimum	Maximum
Entire sample	18,44	5,00	0,00	100,00

Table 17.2 What percentage of the books that you order from academic presses do you order in an eBook format? Broken out by College Type

College Type	Mean	Median	Minimum	Maximum
Public	18,61	5,00	0,00	75,00
Private	18,00	1,00	0,00	100,00

Table 17.3 What percentage of the books that you order from academic presses do you order in an eBook format? Broken out by FTE Enrollment

FTE Enrollment	Mean	Median	Minimum	Maximum
less than 3000	2,78	0,00	0,00	20,00
3000 - 7000	23,00	5,00	0,00	100,00
more than 7000	34,33	35,00	1,00	75,00

Table 17.4 What percentage of the books that you order from academic presses do you order in an eBook format? Broken out by Annual Tuition Level

Annual Tuition Level	Mean	Median	Minimum	Maximum
less than $6000	13,50	0,00	0,00	50,00
$6000 - $20000	22,22	10,00	0,00	75,00
more than $20000	21,00	3,00	0,00	100,00

Table 17.5 What percentage of the books that you order from academic presses do you order in an eBook format? Broken out by Carnegie Class

Carnegie Class	Mean	Median	Minimum	Maximum
Community College / 4-Year College	14,17	2,50	0,00	75,00
MA/PHD Granting / Research University	22,38	10,00	0,00	100,00

What do you think of most of the eBook purchase options offered to you by academic publishers and how might they be altered?

1) Do not like their pricing.
2) Dislike the splintering of platforms and patrons dislike going to multiple places. Aggregators are preferred simply because patrons recognize platforms like EBSCO and ebrary.
3) We would like to purchase the eBook only as a file(s), not depending of the type of the e-book reader.
4) Limited in range particularly of back or older titles, published pre-2011. There seems to be persisting reticence by some academic presses to increase the number of simultaneous users beyond one (1). This is perplexing.
5) We're too small to negotiate with individual publishers.
6) Just starting access this month
7) cost is always an issue - I would like to see customization and better package deals
8) Access should be unlimited for all
9) Many are not available on the DawsonEra or ebrary platforms.
10) Generally speaking, they all need better interfaces. Even the best are still clunky to users.
11) You just changed vocabulary from "academic press" to "academic publisher" so not sure what this question means. Academic publishers like Wiley etc. - just want better prices. We don't pay any attention to eBook sales directly from academic presses - any eBooks we buy from academic presses would go through YBP and we're not tracking which publisher has what options within that, just the platform options (EBL, ebrary, EBSCO, etc.).
12) Currently, all our purchasing in through packages, no individual titles. We like the ownership model, rather than the use model, but only Springer actually does ownership for academic purposes
13) Getting to be very expensive, possibly prohibitively if prices continue to rise
14) They do not meet the needs of my community college students or faculty who overwhelmingly want print books
15) We don't buy individual books
16) Many academic press publishers are just starting to enter the electronic world. We like the JSTOR model. However, we have not seen the demand from our faculty or students as of yet.
17) The academic presses simply do not seem to understand what a number of the larger publishers do: The value of an imprint increases with its exposure and use, and providing advantageous pricing to small institutions (like community colleges) increases awareness and exposure with only minimal increase in system load or even resource use. Consequently, they price the eBooks and collections as though they were selling physical copies (even though they have none of the traditional expenses of physical copies) and yet these small institutions still cannot afford to add the titles to their collections. Even a small increase in subscribers is an increase in revenue... make the pricing fit the customer!

18) I'm not sure what exactly is meant by "academic press" so I estimated. I tried to look at practical vs scholarly, so I included more than just university or society presses. This was a very rough estimate.   I also put 50 for the availability of what we'd like, because I'm trying to say it's hit or miss. I'm not sure what the age is truly.   More reasonable title by title options would be helpful when it's direct with the publisher or through an aggregator. Often the cost for title by title direct with publisher (when the publisher offers subject/pub year sets) are much, much higher than the cost per e-book in a set. I don't expect the title by title price to be as low as the cost per e-book in a set, but not as high as it is now. Especially with reference titles, the cost can be incredibly high.   We prefer working with aggregators, but publishers that have a direct-from-pub option often keep some content to themselves. I'd rather have access to it all on the aggregator platform rather than have to search for it in all different sites.

19) They are ridiculous, inconsistent and aggravating. There should be one or two options. Dealing with licensing agreements that range all over the map makes everybody's jobs harder.

20) would like to own eBook as we own print books

CHAPTER 8 – EBooks in interlibrary loan

Table 18.1 Has the library ever used eBook rental or eBook interlibrary loan sites which enable patrons to have access to an eBook for a fee for a brief specified time period, often 30-60 days?

	No Answer	Yes	No
Entire sample	13,89%	5,56%	80,56%

Table 18.2 Has the library ever used eBook rental or eBook interlibrary loan sites which enable patrons to have access to an eBook for a fee for a brief specified time period, often 30-60 days? Broken out by College Type

College Type	No Answer	Yes	No
Public	8,33%	0,00%	91,67%
Private	25,00%	16,67%	58,33%

Table 18.3 Has the library ever used eBook rental or eBook interlibrary loan sites which enable patrons to have access to an eBook for a fee for a brief specified time period, often 30-60 days? Broken out by FTE Enrollment

FTE Enrollment	No Answer	Yes	No
less than 3000	8,33%	8,33%	83,33%
3000 - 7000	8,33%	0,00%	91,67%
more than 7000	25,00%	8,33%	66,67%

Table 18.4 Has the library ever used eBook rental or eBook interlibrary loan sites which enable patrons to have access to an eBook for a fee for a brief specified time period, often 30-60 days? Broken out by Annual Tuition Level

Annual Tuition Level	No Answer	Yes	No
less than $6000	0,00%	0,00%	100,00%
$6000 - $20000	16,67%	0,00%	83,33%
more than $20000	25,00%	16,67%	58,33%

Table 18.5 Has the library ever used eBook rental or eBook interlibrary loan sites which enable patrons to have access to an eBook for a fee for a brief specified time period, often 30-60 days? Broken out by Carnegie Class

Carnegie Class	No Answer	Yes	No
Community College / 4-Year College	17,65%	0,00%	82,35%
MA/PHD Granting / Research University	10,53%	10,53%	78,95%

Table 19.1 How much did the library spend ($) exclusively on "borrowing rights" to eBooks defined as any model compels you to pay per time borrowed rather than unlimited rights or rights to a certain number of viewings for a set fee?

	Mean	Median	Minimum	Maximum
Entire sample	1440,00	0,00	0,00	31500,00

Table 19.2 How much did the library spend ($) exclusively on "borrowing rights" to eBooks defined as any model compels you to pay per time borrowed rather than unlimited rights or rights to a certain number of viewings for a set fee? Broken out by College Type

College Type	Mean	Median	Minimum	Maximum
Public	264,71	0,00	0,00	3000,00
Private	3937,50	0,00	0,00	31500,00

Table 19.3 How much did the library spend ($) exclusively on "borrowing rights" to eBooks defined as any model compels you to pay per time borrowed rather than unlimited rights or rights to a certain number of viewings for a set fee? Broken out by FTE Enrollment

FTE Enrollment	Mean	Median	Minimum	Maximum
less than 3000	0,00	0,00	0,00	0,00
3000 - 7000	166,67	0,00	0,00	1500,00
more than 7000	5750,00	0,00	0,00	31500,00

Table 19.4 How much did the library spend ($) exclusively on "borrowing rights" to eBooks defined as any model compels you to pay per time borrowed rather than unlimited rights or rights to a certain number of viewings for a set fee? Broken out by Annual Tuition Level

Annual Tuition Level	Mean	Median	Minimum	Maximum
less than $6000	166,67	0,00	0,00	1500,00
$6000 - $20000	428,57	0,00	0,00	3000,00
more than $20000	3500,00	0,00	0,00	31500,00

Table 19.5 How much did the library spend ($) exclusively on "borrowing rights" to eBooks defined as any model compels you to pay per time borrowed rather than unlimited rights or rights to a certain number of viewings for a set fee? Broken out by Carnegie Class

Carnegie Class	Mean	Median	Minimum	Maximum
Community College / 4-Year College	125,00	0,00	0,00	1500,00
MA/PHD Granting / Research University	2653,85	0,00	0,00	31500,00

CHAPTER 9 – Who Uses What

In what areas is your library most anxious to build its eBook collection?

1) Don't know.
2) Health Sciences
3) Health sciences
4) funeral service
5) Nursing, Criminal Justice, Math, Business
6) All
7) For all subjects where the language is other than English. Classics (in Latin, Ancient Greek, Sanskrit, Persian, Arabic) and exegetical texts.
8) health sciences, related to the curriculum
9) Social issues, business, topics for English Comp II
10) Healthcare
11) core collections that support the main curriculum, and new initiatives such as East Asia Studies, Autism Studies, Arabic Studies, and TESOL
12) Social Work, and Part-time courses
13) STEM subjects
14) Law
15) Veterinary, Education
16) Foreign Language, American and English Literature
17) Since we are a science/engineering library that is our focus.
18) In subject those subject areas where online classes are being taught; in those subject areas where the majority of students are working adults who do not come to campus often.
19) Technologies, trades
20) None in particular
21) History, literature
22) Sciences, Allied Health
23) We are anxious to build in areas where demand is present. Sciences, health professions, and general studies.
24) Given our library's growth in this area over the past three years, at this point we are looking to settle in to the large subscription collections we now have & to build our effective use & promotion of these new resources
25) We're a Christian university with a very large online population as well as a good-sized residential population. We are a liberal arts school, but the e-books are definitely selected with the online students in mind. Our most popular online degrees include the DMin, MBA, and EdD. So we are on the lookout for evangelical publishers, especially biblical commentaries. The MBA students also, perhaps surprisingly, use the e-books heavily. And education students do as well. But our

main troublesome area is evangelical publishers, though that has been improving lately.

26) Nursing and allied health (I prefer the word EAGER to anxious.)
27) health sciences

CHAPTER 10 – Use of Tablets in the Library

Table 20.1 Does the library loan out tablet computers to library patrons?

	No Answer	Yes	No	No but in the works
Entire sample	13,89%	22,22%	52,78%	11,11%

Table 20.2 Does the library loan out tablet computers to library patrons? Broken out by College Type

College Type	No Answer	Yes	No	No but in the works
Public	8,33%	16,67%	62,50%	12,50%
Private	25,00%	33,33%	33,33%	8,33%

Table 20.3 Does the library loan out tablet computers to library patrons? Broken out by FTE Enrollment

FTE Enrollment	No Answer	Yes	No	No but in the works
less than 3000	8,33%	33,33%	50,00%	8,33%
3000 - 7000	8,33%	8,33%	66,67%	16,67%
more than 7000	25,00%	25,00%	41,67%	8,33%

Table 20.4 Does the library loan out tablet computers to library patrons? Broken out by Annual Tuition Level

Annual Tuition Level	No Answer	Yes	No	No but in the works
less than $6000	0,00%	16,67%	66,67%	16,67%
$6000 - $20000	16,67%	16,67%	50,00%	16,67%
more than $20000	25,00%	33,33%	41,67%	0,00%

Table 20.5 Does the library loan out tablet computers to library patrons? Broken out by Carnegie Class

Carnegie Class	No Answer	Yes	No	No but in the works
Community College / 4-Year College	17,65%	17,65%	52,94%	11,76%
MA/PHD Granting / Research University	10,53%	26,32%	52,63%	10,53%

Table 21.1 If so, what is the stock of tablet computers that the library maintains for loan?

	Mean	Median	Minimum	Maximum
Entire sample	7,36	4,00	0,00	35,00

Table 21.2 If so what is the stock of tablet computers that the library maintains for loan? Broken out by College Type

College Type	Mean	Median	Minimum	Maximum
Public	8,50	3,50	0,00	35,00
Private	5,83	4,00	0,00	20,00

Table 21.3 If so what is the stock of tablet computers that the library maintains for loan? Broken out by FTE Enrollment

FTE Enrollment	Mean	Median	Minimum	Maximum
less than 3000	5,83	4,00	0,00	20,00
3000 - 7000	2,60	1,00	0,00	6,00
more than 7000	18,33	20,00	0,00	35,00

Table 21.4 If so what is the stock of tablet computers that the library maintains for loan? Broken out by Annual Tuition Level

Annual Tuition Level	Mean	Median	Minimum	Maximum
less than $6000	2,60	1,00	0,00	6,00
$6000 - $20000	14,50	11,50	0,00	35,00
more than $20000	6,40	5,00	0,00	20,00

Table 21.5 If so what is the stock of tablet computers that the library maintains for loan? Broken out by Carnegie Class

Carnegie Class	Mean	Median	Minimum	Maximum
Community College / 4-Year College	9,80	6,00	1,00	35,00
MA/PHD Granting / Research University	6,00	3,00	0,00	20,00

CHAPTER 11 – Print Vs Online

Table 22.1 For approximately what percentage of the eBooks in the library's collection would you estimate that the library also has a corresponding print copy?

	Mean	Median	Minimum	Maximum
Entire sample	17,05	10,00	0,00	100,00

Table 22.2 For approximately what percentage of the eBooks in the library's collection would you estimate that the library also has a corresponding print copy? Broken out by College Type

College Type	Mean	Median	Minimum	Maximum
Public	17,60	8,50	0,00	100,00
Private	15,71	15,00	2,00	50,00

Table 22.3 For approximately what percentage of the eBooks in the library's collection would you estimate that the library also has a corresponding print copy? Broken out by FTE Enrollment

FTE Enrollment	Mean	Median	Minimum	Maximum
less than 3000	11,13	5,00	0,00	50,00
3000 - 7000	16,32	5,00	1,00	95,00
more than 7000	25,20	20,00	4,80	100,00

Table 22.4 For approximately what percentage of the eBooks in the library's collection would you estimate that the library also has a corresponding print copy? Broken out by Annual Tuition Level

Annual Tuition Level	Mean	Median	Minimum	Maximum
less than $6000	7,48	5,00	0,00	25,00
$6000 - $20000	31,90	20,00	4,00	100,00
more than $20000	13,32	4,80	2,00	50,00

Table 22.5 For approximately what percentage of the eBooks in the library's collection would you estimate that the library also has a corresponding print copy? Broken out by Carnegie Class

Carnegie Class	Mean	Median	Minimum	Maximum
Community College / 4-Year College	12,90	5,00	0,80	100,00
MA/PHD Granting / Research University	20,48	15,00	0,00	95,00

Table 23.1 If the library has an endowment, bequest, or specially dedicated fund of any kind for books, may this fund be used for the purchase of eBooks?

	No Answer	Yes, we have a special endowment of other dedicated fund for books but we cannot use it for eBooks	Yes, we have a special endowment or other dedicated fund for books and we can use it for eBooks	No, we have no such endowment or dedicated fund for books of any kind
Entire sample	13,89%	8,33%	30,56%	47,22%

Table 23.2 If the library has an endowment, bequest, or specially dedicated fund of any kind for books, may this fund be used for the purchase of eBooks? Broken out by College Type

College Type	No Answer	Yes, we have a special endowment of other dedicated fund for books but we cannot use it for eBooks	Yes, we have a special endowment or other dedicated fund for books and we can use it for eBooks	No, we have no such endowment or dedicated fund for books of any kind
Public	8,33%	8,33%	33,33%	50,00%
Private	25,00%	8,33%	25,00%	41,67%

Table 23.3 If the library has an endowment, bequest, or specially dedicated fund of any kind for books, may this fund be used for the purchase of eBooks? Broken out by FTE Enrollment

FTE Enrollment	No Answer	Yes, we have a special endowment of other dedicated fund for books but we cannot use it for eBooks	Yes, we have a special endowment or other dedicated fund for books and we can use it for eBooks	No, we have no such endowment or dedicated fund for books of any kind
less than 3000	8,33%	16,67%	25,00%	50,00%
3000 - 7000	8,33%	8,33%	41,67%	41,67%
more than 7000	25,00%	0,00%	25,00%	50,00%

Table 23.4 If the library has an endowment, bequest, or specially dedicated fund of any kind for books, may this fund be used for the purchase of eBooks? Broken out by Annual Tuition Level

Annual Tuition Level	No Answer	Yes, we have a special endowment of other dedicated fund for books but we cannot use it for eBooks	Yes, we have a special endowment or other dedicated fund for books and we can use it for eBooks	No, we have no such endowment or dedicated fund for books of any kind
less than $6000	0,00%	8,33%	33,33%	58,33%
$6000 - $20000	16,67%	8,33%	25,00%	50,00%
more than $20000	25,00%	8,33%	33,33%	33,33%

Table 23.5 If the library has an endowment, bequest, or specially dedicated fund of any kind for books, may this fund be used for the purchase of eBooks? Broken out by Carnegie Class

Carnegie Class	No Answer	Yes, we have a special endowment of other dedicated fund for books but we cannot use it for eBooks	Yes, we have a special endowment or other dedicated fund for books and we can use it for eBooks	No, we have no such endowment or dedicated fund for books of any kind
Community College / 4-Year College	17,65%	11,76%	17,65%	52,94%
MA/PHD Granting / Research University	10,53%	5,26%	42,11%	42,11%

CHAPTER 12 – EBooks and Electronic Course Reserve

Table 24.1 How would you describe your use of eBooks for course reserve?

	No Answer	Not really used at all	Scant use	Used modestly	Significant Use
Entire sample	13,89%	33,33%	33,33%	11,11%	8,33%

Table 24.2 How would you describe your use of eBooks for course reserve? Broken out by College Type

College Type	No Answer	Not really used at all	Scant use	Used modestly	Significant Use
Public	8,33%	33,33%	33,33%	16,67%	8,33%
Private	25,00%	33,33%	33,33%	0,00%	8,33%

Table 24.3 How would you describe your use of eBooks for course reserve? Broken out by FTE Enrollment

FTE Enrollment	No Answer	Not really used at all	Scant use	Used modestly	Significant Use
less than 3000	8,33%	50,00%	25,00%	8,33%	8,33%
3000 - 7000	8,33%	25,00%	41,67%	8,33%	16,67%
more than 7000	25,00%	25,00%	33,33%	16,67%	0,00%

Table 24.4 How would you describe your use of eBooks for course reserve? Broken out by Annual Tuition Level

Annual Tuition Level	No Answer	Not really used at all	Scant use	Used modestly	Significant Use
less than $6000	0,00%	50,00%	25,00%	8,33%	16,67%
$6000 - $20000	16,67%	25,00%	33,33%	25,00%	0,00%
more than $20000	25,00%	25,00%	41,67%	0,00%	8,33%

Table 24.5 How would you describe your use of eBooks for course reserve? Broken out by Carnegie Class

Carnegie Class	No Answer	Not really used at all	Scant use	Used modestly	Significant Use
Community College / 4-Year College	17,65%	47,06%	23,53%	11,76%	0,00%
MA/PHD Granting / Research University	10,53%	21,05%	42,11%	10,53%	15,79%

Over the past two years, the use of eBooks for electronic course reserves has increased or decreased? What are the

1) About the same - very little use.
2) Faculty may assign them directly without going through the library reserve department.
3) Never used them to date.
4) No change. No current or future constraints if faculty would but only use them for reserves.
5) Current constraints are limited the increased demand for it. Limited users and limited chapters available for e-reserves.
6) Increased. Copyright.
7) No remarkable change. There is persisting use of scanned chapters and articles as a labor-intensive task.
8) We do not have much of a course reserve collection; we try to purchase items that would be useful for the curriculum but do not buy electronic textbooks used in class due to our budget.
9) None
10) increased - we are seeing the limited user eBooks being an issue with access
11) Access to an e-reserves module, which is promised for next academic year
12) Increased as academics become more used to the format.
13) Same
14) to go up
15) increased; aggregate instability of titles is a constraint; expect increase in near future
16) management with our ILS, copyright compliance, proxy issues
17) If publishers were more flexible, it would be used more.
18) Two years ago, no eBooks were used for course reserves; now, occasionally, a professor will direct his students to search the catalog and read all or part of an eBook as a class assignment. License and copyright restrictions are current constraints, as is the fact that putting eBooks on course reserve is a new concept for many faculty.
19) Increased, titles we want not available in electronic format
20) Faculty do not embrace eBooks for reserve.
21) we don't use eBooks for reserve
22) increase a small amount
23) At present, this has not impacted us. We would employ EBL (if possible) for reserve use.
24) Increased, definitely. Our main constraint on use is the reluctance of faculty, some of whom like to wax poetic on the feel of turning paper pages....
25) N/A. We don't have electronic course reserves.
26) NA
27) remained the same (low)

CHAPTER 13 – Statistics on EBook Use at the Library

In general how easy is it for you to obtain statistical data and develop reports on eBook use at your library? Is it as easy as for print books?

1) Not easy - takes quite a bit of data manipulation.
2) excellent from EBSCO
3) Same as other databases.
4) Relatively easy.
5) EZ, yes it's as EZ as for database use, or general book circulation data. No we have not had a cooperative eBook arrangement.
6) DIFFICULT! No standardization and difficulty importing different fields. Easier for Databases due to Counter4 & Sushi.
7) Very hard. The vendors don't help us at all.
8) In general it is a complex task. In one case it is downright impossible. I'm referring to EBSCO eBook usage reports which do not distinguish between firm order (approx. 5000 titles) and subscription titles (over 120 000 titles). In another case, that of ebrary and EBL and ProQuest are dragging their feet for any integrated analysis or reports.
9) very difficult -- we have a variety of sources of eBooks and each has a different way to access the data
10) Very difficult. No staff.
11) I find gathering data very easy
12) Easy
13) As easy as database use.
14) Difficult - limited staff time and complicated process
15) Easy
16) Historically it has been very difficult. We just signed a deal with Lexis for eBook usage via Overdrive that promises to provide us with better statistics.
17) Harder than journal title use and much harder than print circ data. Vendors are inconsistent in use of ISBN/eISBN even among their own reports. Also can be hard to separate subscription use from "purchased" use in reports. Nearly impossible to get use based on what year we bought the eBook.
18) EBook vendors are only moderately helpful. It could be easier if everyone complied - with explicit definitions regarding their measurement of Counter standards - with industry standardization and provided all information librarians need to assess their collections holistically - such as providing similar data to a print ILS report. They are not the most helpful in ensuring the right information is provided clearly.
19) It is generally easy for us to obtain COUNTER statistics on eBook usage. Circulation data on print books is more difficult to obtain because queries must be written to extract the data from our ILS.
20) data available but not detailed enough, we want to know how long people spend using an eBook for example, this is not always available

21) EZ to collect from vendor

22) Easy

23) Very cooperative. They want to prove the value of their product.

24) Overall, it is quite hard to create such a report since there are so many publisher/vendor platforms to collect data from. Yes, we do get reports direct from various publishers. ProQuest has a neat new data center for its' e-book platform.

25) Better & more effective & richer understanding of the use of these items than I get from my physical collection's library management software

26) It is basically the same as it is for databases. Some vendors have multiple reports all easily retrieved ourselves. Other vendors have to be contacted or they have to email the reports to us. We prefer being able to collect the data ourselves.

27) It is complicated and unpleasant. EBook vendors are generally cooperative, however.

28) pretty easy

What measures has your library taken to develop easy to develop and easy to use reports on eBook use at your library?

1) We don't have an easy way to measure usage. Right now we print reports and get student workers to tally the number of books in different subject areas by hand. Our light usage allows this.
2) use for annual stats
3) Same use of counter statistics as databases.
4) None, just usage numbers
5) We are trying to find out the best practices of other libraries.
6) We have put the responsibility on to the vendors. Then we complain when they don't develop something for us. Go figure.
7) We haven't taken steps beyond asking our library consortium to assist with this -- they host our ILS, load eBook records, and authenticate our users.
8) In the works
9) None
10) We have one person dedicated to harnessing this data
11) None, use proprietary report structures.
12) None - but new person in post new month should help
13) None
14) Trying to track eBook purchases on a spreadsheet, limited success because too hard to cross-tab our list against vendor usage lists so have to analyze by hand title by title - very time-consuming!
15) Assigning the duty to a single librarian to disseminate.
16) We collect COUNTER statistics and try to present them in a clear, visually appealing format.
17) None, we take what they provide and it meets our needs
18) None
19) Takes time to collect data and I've not found a simple way around that. Otherwise, the data is communicated in multiple venues.
20) We are working on that now. Other than what is supplied by our publishers and vendors, we have not put anything together
21) Not sure what you mean...
22) We do our own manipulation and gathering into spreadsheets, probably like most other libraries. We've pulled from the example of other libraries.
23) In process as I write.
24) we use excel to aggregate numbers we get from providers

Table 25.1 Some eBook vendors do not allow their products to be integrated into a library's systems but instead require that when an eBook link is clicked in a library catalog that the library patron be brought to the eBook vendor's platform in able to access the book. Which phrase describes your feelings about this?

	No Answer	It is natural that the publisher would want to retain some control	It's slightly inconvenient but not really a problem for us	It's problematic and we would like to see this changed soon	It's a major issue for us and we have or might withhold business from vendors that do it
Entire sample	19,44%	22,22%	25,00%	5,56%	27,78%

Table 25.2 Some eBook vendors do not allow their products to be integrated into a library's systems but instead require that when an eBook link is clicked in a library catalog that the library patron be brought to the eBook vendor's platform in able to access the book. Which phrase describes your feelings about this? Broken out by College Type

College Type	No Answer	It is natural that the publisher would want to retain some control	It's slightly inconvenient but not really a problem for us	It's problematic and we would like to see this changed soon	It's a major issue for us and we have or might withhold business from vendors that do it
Public	16,67%	25,00%	29,17%	8,33%	20,83%
Private	25,00%	16,67%	16,67%	0,00%	41,67%

Table 25.3 Some eBook vendors do not allow their products to be integrated into a library's systems but instead require that when an eBook link is clicked in a library catalog that the library patron be brought to the eBook vendor's platform in able to access the book. Which phrase describes your feelings about this? Broken out by FTE Enrollment

FTE Enrollment	No Answer	It is natural that the publisher would want to retain some control	It's slightly inconvenient but not really a problem for us	It's problematic and we would like to see this changed soon	It's a major issue for us and we have or might withhold business from vendors that do it
less than 3000	8,33%	8,33%	33,33%	0,00%	50,00%
3000 - 7000	16,67%	25,00%	25,00%	8,33%	25,00%
more than 7000	33,33%	33,33%	16,67%	8,33%	8,33%

Table 25.4 Some eBook vendors do not allow their products to be integrated into a library's systems but instead require that when an eBook link is clicked in a library catalog that the library patron be brought to the eBook vendor's platform in able to access the book. Which phrase describes your feelings about this? Broken out by Annual Tuition Level

Annual Tuition Level	No Answer	It is natural that the publisher would want to retain some control	It's slightly inconvenient but not really a problem for us	It's problematic and we would like to see this changed soon	It's a major issue for us and we have or might withhold business from vendors that do it
less than $6000	0,00%	41,67%	16,67%	8,33%	33,33%
$6000 - $20000	33,33%	8,33%	50,00%	8,33%	0,00%
more than $20000	25,00%	16,67%	8,33%	0,00%	50,00%

Table 25.5 Some eBook vendors do not allow their products to be integrated into a library's systems but instead require that when an eBook link is clicked in a library catalog that the library patron be brought to the eBook vendor's platform in able to access the book. Which phrase describes your feelings about this? Broken out by Carnegie Class

Carnegie Class	No Answer	It is natural that the publisher would want to retain some control	It's slightly inconvenient but not really a problem for us	It's problematic and we would like to see this changed soon	It's a major issue for us and we have or might withhold business from vendors that do it
Community College / 4-Year College	23,53%	17,65%	29,41%	5,88%	23,53%
MA/PHD Granting / Research University	15,79%	26,32%	21,05%	5,26%	31,58%

CHAPTER 14 – EDirectories

Table 26.1 How much did the library in the past year spend ($) on electronic/internet versions of directories?

	Mean	Median	Minimum	Maximum
Entire sample	2259,96	0,00	0,00	25079,00

Table 26.2 How much did the library in the past year spend ($) on electronic/internet versions of directories? Broken out by College Type

College Type	Mean	Median	Minimum	Maximum
Public	2798,76	0,00	0,00	25079,00
Private	1242,22	0,00	0,00	10000,00

Table 26.3 How much did the library in the past year spend ($) on electronic/internet versions of directories? Broken out by FTE Enrollment

FTE Enrollment	Mean	Median	Minimum	Maximum
less than 3000	909,09	0,00	0,00	10000,00
3000 - 7000	3631,00	0,00	0,00	25079,00
more than 7000	2680,00	540,00	0,00	12000,00

Table 26.4 How much did the library in the past year spend ($) on electronic/internet versions of directories? Broken out by Annual Tuition Level

Annual Tuition Level	Mean	Median	Minimum	Maximum
less than $6000	1772,73	0,00	0,00	12000,00
$6000 - $20000	4011,29	0,00	0,00	25079,00
more than $20000	1397,50	0,00	0,00	10000,00

Table 26.5 How much did the library in the past year spend ($) on electronic/internet versions of directories? Broken out by Carnegie Class

Carnegie Class	Mean	Median	Minimum	Maximum
Community College / 4-Year College	584,62	0,00	0,00	7500,00
MA/PHD Granting / Research University	3935,31	0,00	0,00	25079,00

Table 27.1 How much does the library plan to spend ($) on electronic/internet versions of directories in the upcoming year?

	Mean	Median	Minimum	Maximum
Entire sample	2065,15	0,00	0,00	25079,00

Table 27.2 How much does the library plan to spend ($) on electronic/internet versions of directories in the upcoming year? Broken out by College Type

College Type	Mean	Median	Minimum	Maximum
Public	2476,61	0,00	0,00	25079,00
Private	1242,22	0,00	0,00	10000,00

Table 27.3 How much does the library plan to spend ($) on electronic/internet versions of directories in the upcoming year? Broken out by FTE Enrollment

FTE Enrollment	Mean	Median	Minimum	Maximum
less than 3000	909,09	0,00	0,00	10000,00
3000 - 7000	3575,44	0,00	0,00	25079,00
more than 7000	1940,00	0,00	0,00	12000,00

Table 27.4 How much does the library plan to spend ($) on electronic/internet versions of directories in the upcoming year? Broken out by Annual Tuition Level

Annual Tuition Level	Mean	Median	Minimum	Maximum
less than $6000	1727,27	0,00	0,00	12000,00
$6000 - $20000	3197,38	0,00	0,00	25079,00
more than $20000	1397,50	0,00	0,00	10000,00

Table 27.5 How much does the library plan to spend ($) on electronic/internet versions of directories in the upcoming year? Broken out by Carnegie Class

Carnegie Class	Mean	Median	Minimum	Maximum
Community College / 4-Year College	546,15	0,00	0,00	7000,00
MA/PHD Granting / Research University	3475,64	0,00	0,00	25079,00

CHAPTER 15 – Pricing

Table 28 In the past year what has been the library's experience with changes in the prices of eBooks relative to the changes in price of traditional print books, online databases of full text articles, and other resources specified below?

Table 28.1.1 In the past year what has been the library's experience with changes in the prices of eBooks relative to print books?

	No Answer	Price increases have been about the same	Price increases have been higher for eBooks	Our eBook prices have not increased
Entire sample	22,22%	38,89%	30,56%	8,33%

Table 28.1.2 In the past year what has been the library's experience with changes in the prices of eBooks relative to print books? Broken out by College Type

College Type	No Answer	Price increases have been about the same	Price increases have been higher for eBooks	Our eBook prices have not increased
Public	16,67%	37,50%	37,50%	8,33%
Private	33,33%	41,67%	16,67%	8,33%

Table 28.1.3 In the past year what has been the library's experience with changes in the prices of eBooks relative to print books? Broken out by FTE Enrollment

FTE Enrollment	No Answer	Price increases have been about the same	Price increases have been higher for eBooks	Our eBook prices have not increased
less than 3000	16,67%	58,33%	16,67%	8,33%
3000 - 7000	16,67%	33,33%	50,00%	0,00%
more than 7000	33,33%	25,00%	25,00%	16,67%

Table 28.1.4 In the past year what has been the library's experience with changes in the prices of eBooks relative to print books? Broken out by Annual Tuition Level

Annual Tuition Level	No Answer	Price increases have been about the same	Price increases have been higher for eBooks	Our eBook prices have not increased
less than $6000	0,00%	41,67%	50,00%	8,33%
$6000 - $20000	41,67%	33,33%	16,67%	8,33%
more than $20000	25,00%	41,67%	25,00%	8,33%

Table 28.1.5 In the past year what has been the library's experience with changes in the prices of eBooks relative to print books? Broken out by Carnegie Class

Carnegie Class	No Answer	Price increases have been about the same	Price increases have been higher for eBooks	Our eBook prices have not increased
Community College / 4-Year College	23,53%	35,29%	35,29%	5,88%
MA/PHD Granting / Research University	21,05%	42,11%	26,32%	10,53%

Table 28.2.1 In the past year what has been the library's experience with changes in the prices of eBooks relative to online full text databases?

	No Answer	Price increases have been about the same	Price increases have been higher for eBooks	Our eBook prices have not increased
Entire sample	27,78%	58,33%	8,33%	5,56%

Table 28.2.2 In the past year what has been the library's experience with changes in the prices of eBooks relative to online full text databases? Broken out by College Type

College Type	No Answer	Price increases have been about the same	Price increases have been higher for eBooks	Our eBook prices have not increased
Public	25,00%	62,50%	8,33%	4,17%
Private	33,33%	50,00%	8,33%	8,33%

Table 28.2.3 In the past year what has been the library's experience with changes in the prices of eBooks relative to online full text databases? Broken out by FTE Enrollment

FTE Enrollment	No Answer	Price increases have been about the same	Price increases have been higher for eBooks	Our eBook prices have not increased
less than 3000	25,00%	66,67%	0,00%	8,33%
3000 - 7000	25,00%	58,33%	16,67%	0,00%
more than 7000	33,33%	50,00%	8,33%	8,33%

Table 28.2.4 In the past year what has been the library's experience with changes in the prices of eBooks relative to online full text databases? Broken out by Annual Tuition Level

Annual Tuition Level	No Answer	Price increases have been about the same	Price increases have been higher for eBooks	Our eBook prices have not increased
less than $6000	8,33%	75,00%	8,33%	8,33%
$6000 - $20000	41,67%	50,00%	8,33%	0,00%
more than $20000	33,33%	50,00%	8,33%	8,33%

Table 28.2.5 In the past year what has been the library's experience with changes in the prices of eBooks relative to online full text databases? Broken out by Carnegie Class

Carnegie Class	No Answer	Price increases have been about the same	Price increases have been higher for eBooks	Our eBook prices have not increased
Community College / 4-Year College	29,41%	52,94%	11,76%	5,88%
MA/PHD Granting / Research University	26,32%	63,16%	5,26%	5,26%

Table 29.1 What was the average percentage change in eBook prices that your organization paid in the last year?

	Mean	Median	Minimum	Maximum
Entire sample	9,19	5,00	0,00	45,00

Table 29.2 What was the average percentage change in eBook prices that your organization paid in the last year? Broken out by College Type

College Type	Mean	Median	Minimum	Maximum
Public	9,47	5,00	0,00	45,00
Private	8,50	7,50	2,00	15,00

Table 29.3 What was the average percentage change in eBook prices that your organization paid in the last year? Broken out by FTE Enrollment

FTE Enrollment	Mean	Median	Minimum	Maximum
less than 3000	4,57	5,00	0,00	10,00
3000 - 7000	8,50	5,00	0,00	20,00
more than 7000	15,50	10,00	4,00	45,00

Table 29.4 What was the average percentage change in eBook prices that your organization paid in the last year? Broken out by Annual Tuition Level

Annual Tuition Level	Mean	Median	Minimum	Maximum
less than $6000	5,78	4,00	0,00	20,00
$6000 - $20000	15,00	7,50	5,00	45,00
more than $20000	8,50	7,50	2,00	15,00

Table 29.5 What was the average percentage change in eBook prices that your organization paid in the last year? Broken out by Carnegie Class

Carnegie Class	Mean	Median	Minimum	Maximum
Community College / 4-Year College	7,25	5,00	0,00	20,00
MA/PHD Granting / Research University	10,38	5,00	0,00	45,00

CHAPTER 16 – EBook Collection Planning

Discuss your library's eBook collection strategy. How fast do you expect your eBook collection to grow?

1) We rely completely on a consortium at this point. We would like to increase spending on eBooks as well as print but budget constraints have not allowed this.

2) We only purchase EBSCO eBook collections at this time

3) Our usage has not grown at the same rate as the national average. In the health professions, our usage is more electronic than print. Patrons seem to be able to search eBooks adequately. We catalog eBooks the same as print, individually or in aggregates. Information literacy has focused on Google and not eBooks.

4) Patrons haven't expressed a great deal of interest in eBooks yet, but I know they are the future and we are starting to develop our collection in anticipation of their more widespread acceptance.

5) We do not have a strategy yet but may have to in the next 2 years.

6) EBook collections are growing rapidly. It is replacing money we would have spent on print books since patrons in MANY cases prefer e-books (i.e. less unavailability and accessible at 3am when they start their paper/research). We still have certain subject areas that prefer print and other subject areas frequently do not have books available as e-books.

7) We expect our eBook collection will grow depending on the adjustment of the business models to library workflows. The cataloging will be the same and information literacy easier to provide.

8) The strategy appears to be to match the number of print with the number of eBooks. This should place the library in a virtual space where physical use of a collection diminishes. This is driven by the ubiquity of devices and the opportunity to *push* titles to our users. We also have a space issue and in creating learning commons, we can consolidate and reduce shelving. The library policy is to buy eBooks and streaming over analogue and print where ever possible. The commitment to eBooks in technical services has resulted in outsourced or purchased cataloguing or *metadata services* to manage the discovery aspects but not the Authority or WorldCat holdings aspects. Information literacy strategies have been neglected (discounted) as it is fashionable to say that GenY wants to do it all by keyword so the library should not interfere.

9) We have reduced spending on traditional books and hope to continue the trend significantly. The search capacity is one of the benefits. Because we have so many PDA records, information literacy strategies are tricky -- we don't want to click on an eBook returned in any patron's search *only* to show the patron how to use it, lest we be charged for an unwanted item. We are hoping the eBook collection will grow significantly, particularly in curriculum areas where we have a lot of distance learning, general education courses, or theft of items (e.g., medical).

10) I will buy all I can afford that instructors guarantee me will be used. Already spending much less on print books to pay for databases and technology.

11) As we weed we are looking to see if the print is in an e format to move everything to an eBook. We are running out of space so having the book in the eFormat allows us to keep the book in some way

12) eBook mostly bought via aggregated databases; yes, it has reduced spending on print resources; more is being spent on live-streaming mediate though. Library Instruction sessions include effective searching and identifying eBooks, and special workshops are held for these eBooks databases

13) We tend to purchase eBooks as a back-up to the print versions, we are a small university and need to make the most of the limited funds that we have. Our subscription to the ebrary service gives us a base from which to promote eBook usage, and our use of DwasonEra allows us to fill in the gaps for subject specific materials. Through DawsonEra we also have access to the full collection (350,000 titles) which our patrons can then ask us to 'rent' for them on a weekly basis. This has proved popular with approximately 250 individual rentals this academic year.

14) We spend a lot of money but I don't think our patrons like eBooks and often make comments they would rather we have hard copy. This is difficult as we have many students who do not come onto main site so eBooks, you would think, would be well used, but they are not.

15) Our students make faces when we point them to eBooks. We haven't focused on them because we don't have the demand. Should that change, we will change our strategy. Currently everything we have comes as part of a huge consortia package that is primarily databases but also contains eBooks.

16) I expect out eBook collection to grow exponentially over the next 5 years. It hasn't yet but will eventually force a reduction in spending on print books. EBooks are in our catalog so searched with print simultaneously.

17) Each subject librarian free to make their own strategy - some favor eBooks (Health, Veterinary, Education, Sociology), some refuse to buy them (English, History). Expect collection to grow because of aggregate packages more than individual purchases. Same budget as print books so definitely decrease in print spending as result. Patrons definitely search within eBooks in EDS (EBSCO) but probably not deliberately so. No effect yet on cataloguing, mixed info lit based on individual liaison librarians as above.

18) It appears our patrons do make use of eBook searching capacity, as we still load all marc records into our OPAC rather than letting our discovery service provide links. This has led to a small but measureable decline in print circulation starting in 2014 and this will be met with a larger portion of money for eBooks come the start of the upcoming fiscal year and a slight decline in print spending. EBooks have changed our information literacy strategy in that we will demo only eBook navigation, rather than article navigation, through our discovery product or OPAC in classes and in video.

19) Our strategy has been to acquire books in the preferred format of the requester, print or electronic.

20) when program is offered on multiple campuses eBook format preferred, students still reluctant to use eBooks, everyone still seems to want to read in print, but the convenience of obtaining the eBook is good, but then users are printing pages

21) We will only add what faculty direct us to add in eBook format given that they are so reluctant to embrace the format. We address it in faculty development workshops and teach it in information literacy classes but the usage stays relatively lower than our expectations.

22) Students don't use eBooks very much, except for the nursing books from STAT REF. Despite our having 150,000 or so books available, students prefer the printed book

23) We have a balanced approach. We purchase books because students still prefer printed books. However, we are purchasing e-books to provide off-campus access.

24) Our present strategy is to be cautious with e-books, as the academic publishers are still behind what is offered to the public libraries - plus there are so many issues with DRM's (requiring additional software such as Adobe Digital Editions) that hamper full adoption by users. We are also frustrated by pricing practices of publishers and see many publishers that have problematic or archaic e-book interfaces. We are having problems with cataloging e-books as we have subscriptions, DDA profiles, and permanent purchases - yet none are accurately reflected in the Library's catalog. In the long run, we see this as problematic; especially when profiles come and go and we need to know about this in case have questions from users or administrators.

25) Our eBook collections are expanding as fast as I can afford to make them; it has led to some reduced spending on physical books because I get nearly 9x the usage from digital resources than do from the physical collection. Not sure what you mean about eBook searching capacity: those title are listed alongside physical titles in our library as through there were no difference. Most of our eBooks are simply format changes to physical book titles - format changes do not affect cataloging or information literacy teaching or strategies in any deeply significant way.

26) Spending on both print and e-books is going up. We are a relatively young institution, founded in 1971. We are in a better financial situation lately, so we are making numerous retrospective print book purchases. This will continue for a few more years, and then the expectation is for demand for print to decrease. E-book demand will increase. This is also true because we have a very large online population - larger than our residential. E-books are extremely useful to those students so we invest heavily in e-books already. We have an E-Resource Cataloging Librarian specifically for e-books and streaming media cataloging mainly. There has been one staff person underneath this librarian, but we just got 2 more staff positions approved. In terms of information literacy, we include e-books in much of the instruction, especially for online students. We also try to educate faculty on e-books and how to use them. We also have a LibGuide dedicated to helping students use the library e-books.

27) Our patrons are resistant. So are our faculty. Given the slump in usage, we cancelled an eBook subscription package for FY 2015.

28) We would like to grow our eBook collection, but our users are resistant, both faculty and students. As much as literature stresses the computer savviness of young people, our students request print books and when presented with an eBook

alternative for a title the library does not own in print, most students will see if they can either buy or ILL the print version. They are not enamored with the capability of searching in eBooks.

CHAPTER 17 – ETextbooks

Describe your library's attempts to license eTextbooks? Have you approached or negotiated with any textbook publishers over eBook

1) None
2) NA
3) Not yet.
4) No
5) We have not tried this.
6) No. Our policy is to not purchase textbooks used in courses.
7) We don't have any attempts like this yet.
8) Nil
9) We have not attempted to license traditional eTextbooks because there is a separate eTextbook initiative on campus. We have tried to license Facts & Comparisons for our pharmacy tech students to the benefit of other health science students, but the cost was prohibitive.
10) we have an eBookstore that we use - luckily we do not need to do this
11) N/a
12) No plans.
13) Not applicable
14) n/a
15) We have not dealt with this issue.
16) No
17) no attempts to date, no strategy
18) 0 attempts, we feel this would have to be a conversation started above the library.
19) We have not begun to license e Textbooks yet. Since our policy is to not purchase textbooks in print, it is unlikely that we will begin to do so in the near future.
20) Would like to see more titles available first
21) No attempts
22) Have not done this. We are a textbook depository for the state of Tennessee and few of the textbooks are offered as eBooks.
23) We are not in the business of buy textbooks and will not migrate to purchasing e-textbooks. Our students have been vocal about not desiring e-textbooks.
24) No, our library does not collect textbooks in any manner. The university book store is responsible for this.
25) We generally do not collect textbooks, so we have not attempted anything in this area.
26) We will purchase e-books which are used as textbooks in classes on occasion. We do not intentionally seek it out for the most part. Usually a traditional textbook is not available as an e-book to the library. What we do get is usually not intended for use as a textbook or supplementary reading to a class.

27) I refuse to license textbooks. We are exploring OER, and I hope the eBook publishers that hold libraries hostage all go out of business.

28) none

Made in the USA
Lexington, KY
29 September 2015